PART I-NORBERT

Chapter 1

Brilliant white rushed around her.

"Welcome to the Expiation Zone. We're so glad to have you here!"

"Where—?" Everything was a little too bright, a little too hazy.

"Just take it easy, Sugar. I'm Patricia, your Resident Guide, but you can call me 'Patty.' You can ask me for anything, and I'll help you if I can. We're going to make sure your stay here in the E.Z. is as pleasant as can be. Mmmmm. Did you hear that, Norbert? It's going to be a good day! I'm rhyming already! 'E.Z. and 'can be!'"

Patty? I don't think I know a Pat—"Where am—?"

"Just don't you worry your pretty head about it, Sugar. What you're feelin' right now is completely natural. Oooh, so young yet, too. Norbert! Norbert, come on over here! This is a fine match for you! It's your lucky day! You two are going to get along just fine! Not like that old spinster from last month. Mmmm, I think this is a match made in Heaven for you, Norbert!"

"Where—?" She couldn't recall where she was or how she had gotten there. She was mostly aware of a lightness. A feeling of weightlessness that surrounded her, or was it just the absence of heaviness? There was no weight to anything: arms, legs, feet. She felt as if she was able to float, but still grounded by something she couldn't see or feel, like a Macy's Day parade balloon parked and staged before the big show. Suddenly, a large, dark figure came into view as her eyes began to focus on a hazy shape in front of her.

"There you are! Norbert! Norbert, quit lollygagging and get on over here. You're going to like this one! She's pretty!"

Another hazy shape entered her field of vision, this one leaner and not as tall. "Lord, Patricia. I heard you the first time. And you know that I don't especially care what our cadets look like—that last one you sent me could have modeled for *GQ* and look at the way that whole mess turned out—Oh, she's stirring," Norbert continued with vague interest. "You were right, Patricia, she is rather a catch. Poor thing...unlucky right up until the end. And Lord knows it's not going to get too much better here with me. Hello there, Darling," Norbert purred. His voice was like a cat's buzz. Or like the way that a voice actor would use if he were playing a cat or a lion in a movie. Flamboyant. Experienced. Snide. Yet, smooth.

"Where am I?" the hoarse words clanked out of her mouth, the stopped and rusty train finally getting enough momentum to plunge forward. Jennifer focused intently on what looked like two people in front of her. The first was a middle-aged woman, large of build with brightly colored lips that formed a genuine smile on her regal, smooth hazelnut brown face. Her wild black hair reached both up to the sky and down to touch her shoulders where it grazed her royal blue top, which looked like it belonged to a set of scrubs.

Scrubs. An idea entered her unsteady mind. "Am I in the hospital?" Jennifer asked groggily, eyeing the woman closely. She was wearing a badge around her neck like the ones that nurses wear. *I must be in the hospital.*

"MmmmmNnnnnnn. No, Sweetie, you're past the hospital, Sugar, but not that far. You're in the middle here. The E.Z. I like to call it 'The Big E.Z' 'cause it reminds me of my hometown, ain't that right, Mr. Norbert?"

"Mmmmhhhhmmm." Norbert filed his nail with an emery board, disinterested.

"The...middle...?" Jennifer's eyes focused on the jaded person standing next to Patty. He must have been the proprietor of the cat-voice. He was shorter than the woman, old, but with sparkling green eyes that glimmered with the diamond dance of corrected cataracts. He wore a blonde hairpiece that looked more befitting for a game show host as it betrayed the shape of his head and his natural hair coloring, which snuck out at the sides and back. Despite the untamed and comical hair, he wore a neat black suit and shirt that was impeccably pressed, and his expertly knotted tie was secured with a horseshoe tie-pin.

"There she is." The voice purred with genuine interest. There was a coziness to its rough cadence. "Howya doin', there, Darling? I'm so sorry for your loss. I think you might have had a rough crash-landing by the looks of it. Not what you were expecting, huh?"

Jennifer thought maybe the man could be a doctor, but there was something less surgical, less sterile about his demeanor. Plus, he smelled so strongly of cigarettes and soothing cologne...and nothing of the insipid bareness that she typically associated with doctors seemed to surround him. He had the demeanor of fine polishing and good rearing, but there was an asperity to him that negated the professionalism that she'd seen in most doctors. Not that she was an expert. She tried to remember the last time that she had been to a doctor's office but was cut off again by Patty's voice breaking into her thoughts.

"Let's just get some of this clerical work out of the way here, Sugar. Jennifer Uccello? Am I saying that correctly? Cello? Like the instrument?" Jennifer shook her head absently in confused agreement. "Okay, then." Patty's voice continued on, "Age: 26. Birthdate: oh-six-two-six nineteen ninety-two. 5'3" tall. Eyes: Brown. Roman Catholic. Divorced. No children. Royal Crest School of Cosmetology. Youngstown, Ohio."

"That's…that's me," Jennifer broke in. "What hospital is this?" she asked as she surveyed the white, barren walls. For all its clinical qualities, her surroundings still did not strike her as a place where there were sick people. Or cures. There was no beeping. No sense of urgency. No clocks.

"This isn't a hospital, Sugar. You're a few steps away from the Empire. So close, you can almost taste it. Poor thing! You mustn't be too lucky because you don't look to be the terrible type, and you probably just had a bad couple of days. I can tell that a mile away, can't I, Norbert? 'Member last time when I pegged that guy right down to the date for his last two days? I think he thought I must've been stalking him for how on the nose I nailed it with that one; ain't that right, Norbert?"

"Hmmm…oh, yes, Patricia…you're a regular gumshoe." Norbert's green eyes rolled in scorn, but Jennifer detected slight curiosity amid the disdain and boredom that seemed to be emanating from the reserved man. "Why don't you give Jennifer the spiel instead of keeping our poor little Ms. Uccello waiting here in wonder?"

"Well, Sugar, you are in a bit of luck here! Your passing has found you in the Expiation Zone."

"My pass—?"

"It looks like your last day was…" she flipped quickly through a thin stack of paperwork that she removed from a manila dossier, "three days ago, and you have swiftly moved along the river path to being a Rev. 20. Revelation 20s are the judged interveners. The 'Bridge to the Empire.' Norbert, get me my book, please. I see you're a Catholic, Ms. Uccello, so I'll just…" Patricia rifled through pages of what looked like a giant encyclopedia, earmarked with different-colored ribbons sticking out of various pages. "Let's see…Baptist, Hindu, Islamic, Primal-Indigenous—"

"That was a fun one," Norbert broke in. "I had a good time with that indigenous one. I wonder what ever happened to that poor soul…I honestly think I lost him somewhere along the way before the end of our last mission—what with running from all those tigers and shit…" He began to laugh to himself as if remembering.

"That's enough out of you, Norbert! Now…here we go," Patty adjusted her reading glasses to sit at the end of her smooth nose and began quoting from the large text, '"And I saw the dead, great and small, standing before the throne, and the books were opened. Another book was opened, which is the book of life. The dead were judged according to what they had done as recorded in the books.'" She closed the book with a sense of finality.

As if that makes any sense.

Sensing Jennifer's confusion, Patty picked up, "That's from Revelation 20:12…hence the name 'Rev 20s'."

Still lost. "I'm…" Jennifer glanced around slowly, focusing on as much as she could. The fogginess and haziness were replaced with acute perception, as if she could hear, smell, and see better than she had ever been able to before. She looked down at her hands, her feet. Her clothes. She was dressed particularly nicely in a form-fitting black dress. She felt her head and could tell that her shining dark brown hair was twisted up in a styled knot. She ran her hands along her ears and touched the diamond stud earrings that her grandmother had left her when she died. Her good jewelry. Her only good jewelry. "I'm…not alive anymore?"

"Mmmmnnnnnn. Nope. No, Sugar, you are dead. Departed. Deceased. Defunct."

"I think the dossier listed 'English' as her preferred language, Patricia. We don't need to belabor the point, showing your newfound posthumous skills with the pocket thesaurus."

"Norbert, Sweetie, we've been doing this together long enough. You know that's just the way I am by now. And you know you can call me 'Patty.'"

"Oh, I do, Darling," Norbert grumbled as an aside to Jennifer. "I just replace that 'P' with a big, ole 'F' and I usually don't say it to her face…"

"What's that now, Mr. Norbert?"

"Oh, nothing, dear…you just go on and give little Miss Jennifer here the lowdown. If you need me, I'll be in my office." Norbert disappeared down a long corridor.

"He has an office?" Jennifer asked, uncertain of everything at this point and trying to piece together what might be happening.

"That's where he goes and smokes his cigarettes, Sweetie. That man spends more time puffing and not enough time doing his work. Lord, I swear he's never going to get out of this place the way he's been dragging his feet around here and leaving me to do—"

"Where is 'around here'? I'm sorry. I—you were saying—I'm not alive anymore. The E.Z.? Am I…Is this…this is Heaven?" She had a difficult time hiding her disappointment in the bland surroundings, the lack of feeling, the eclectic mix of odd and complete strangers.

"God no, Sugar! No…it's like I was saying. This is a little stop along the way. There's that big, old record book I was telling you about, Baby, where all your earthly works are recorded throughout your life. We gotta sort a few of those pages out for you, Miss Jennifer." A faraway look entered Patricia's usually charismatic eyes. "We all of us got to sort those pages out, tear up a few bad ones, write new ones, help some other folks out along the way, and then we'll be off to that Empire you hear so much about when you're going through life."

A book? "So...my *book*...my life...at the end of it all...why am I here? Did I do something wrong? I wasn't a bad person..."

"It's not your life, Jennifer. Let me tell you something sad and true, child. It is not your life that gets you to Heaven. Or to Hell. Or even here in the Expiation Zone. It's five days."

"Five days?"

Patty nodded her head once. "Five days. And this here is your chance to turn the tide and shimmy on out of here and get to where you belong."

Chapter 2

A nagging question tugged at Jennifer. "How did I die?" she asked Patty, her thin, dark brows knitted in concern.

"Mmmmnnnnn. Can't help you there, Sugar. Nope. That's everyone's first question, and that's the only one we can't answer," Patty admitted, shaking her head sadly.

Jennifer watched Patty's hair sway as she shook her head. "Why can't you tell me?" she implored, somewhat hurt and still quite ill-at-ease as a result of the confusion and uncertainty of where she was, how she got here, and what she was doing.

"I would if I could, Sugar. But I can't. Up here, no one knows how anybody died. We could guess..." Patty looked down at her royal blue scrubs. "I must have been at work, taking care of Miss. Culpepper. It must have been a Wednesday cause I wore my blue scrubs on Wednesdays and my purple ones on Thursdays, and then on Fridays, I would get wild and just wear the ones with tiger designs...old Miss. Culpepper—she hated Fridays...and most other days, too—"

Patty continued gaily on her discourse regarding the schedule shared between her and Miss. Culpepper while Jennifer looked down again at her black dress and heels. This was the outfit that she kept in her closet for funerals mostly when one of her older clients passed away. As a hairdresser, practically everything that she owned was black. Black jeans, black tops, black flats. It was no big surprise that she'd be wearing black now, but she didn't wear dresses much at all, and wearing heels to work cutting hair for eight hours a shift was asking for trouble and a backache.

"—I couldn't help but wonder if I maybe took a heart attack liftin' ol' Miss. Culpepper outta one of those deep bubble baths she liked to take, but she didn't take bubble baths on a Wednesday. She liked to do that on a Friday morning after her coffee and right before I took her to Lady Barbara's to get her hair done— seeing's how she only went out of the house once a week and she didn't like to get her hair too wet getting in and out of that tub. Lord, she would stay in there until her pruney hands would get wrinkles on top of wrinkles—"

Jennifer examined her own hands and fingernails. She ran a curious finger along her face and neck and gingerly patted the top of her hair. She let her tongue explore along each tooth in her mouth. She wiggled her toes as best she could in the pointed space of her heels. At the surface level, everything seemed as it was before...Another question entered her mind as she tried to piece together her surroundings. "Who's Norbert?"

Patty abruptly broke out of her ramblings. "Oh, Sugar. Norbert's your mentor. He's a Rev. 20, too. Same as you. He's going to teach you what you need to do to leave the E.Z. and get to your final harbor. I don't envy you, though, Sugar. Norbert's been here longer than anybody can remember, and I don't think he's in any hurry to leave the E.Z. Probably afraid there won't be a smoking section in the last terminal for all I know. His last four charges quit on him and asked to be moved on to someone else. He's an agreeable sort, but it takes a special initiate to really understand Norbert, Sugar. And I think you're just the one to do it, too!"

Jennifer thought of the eccentric man in the black suit wearing the ill-fitting toupee. *What could he teach me?* Patty noticed the way that Jennifer's eyebrows were knit together and forced herself to try to be as clear as possible in her explanation. "I think I need to back up a little bit here, Sugar. It's like I was saying earlier about those five days. Here, have a seat." Patty motioned to a white chair with her supple brown fingers and then inched her chair closer to Jennifer as she explained. "My mama always used to say, 'Nobody ever comes back to tell us what happens when we die,' so I'll tell you: You die. And that..." her brown hands spread wide in demonstration as she spoke, "...newly released energy needs to go someplace. Every religion has a different way of telling it, and mine might be different from yours...and there's people who don't believe in anything at all...but believe me—we are all just energy that needs to go someplace. Where you wind up doesn't have as much to do with what you did all throughout your life as it has to do with five days of your life. Five days—completely chosen at random—that's was determines your little Shangri-la, Sugar. Call it 'Heaven.' Call it 'Nirvana.' Call it whatever you want—it's five days that get you there. Now, if your whole life was spent cultivatin' some wicked and bad energy—you know the type: your terrorists, hackers, big heartless bullies—if you spent your whole life being rotten, statistically, your five randomly chosen days were probably rotten, too. And you know where that gets you, right, Sugar?"

Jennifer nodded slowly, her eyes narrowing as she studied Patty and concluded that she was telling the truth—or, at least, as much of it as she knew herself.

"—Eternal damnation! Hooo...I don't even like to say it! Then, you have your folks who've spent their whole lives just tending to that good ole crop of positive energy: your NICU nurses, kindergarten teachers, emergency responders—the numbers are on their side that their five random days are going to be spent doing something of merit. Something righteous. Something deserving of an eternity of playing real-life Candyland in the sky 'cause they've been caught doing something good on each of their five days."

"Is that what Heaven is? Candyland?"

"I don't know, Sugar. Like I said, nobody done come back to tell *me* what happened to 'em when they left. I've got a feeling mine and yours is different. I've got a feeling mine and that poor aborigine Norbert scared off a few weeks ago is different, too. Lord knows, mine has got to be different than Norbert's 'cause I don't aim to spend my eternity coughing myself to death trying to breathe while he puffs on those cancer-causing coffin nails of his— and he can't be around me for longer than ten minutes before he tenses up and goes stormin' off to his 'office', complaining that I talk too loud and too much, so I don't imagine his version is anything like mine. 'Course, I do like to talk, and I don't expect to fill my days up in silent meditation. Mmmmm...but I know when I get to wherever I'm going, I'm gonna see my mama and have me the biggest bowl of her gumbo, and it's gonna be like Mardi Gras every single day with some zydeco music, and a cool breeze cuttin' through some sweet, muggy air hanging heavy on a night that never ends..."

None of what Patty was saying seemed to appeal to Jennifer. *Different Heavens for everyone*. Jennifer thought of how most of the women with naturally curly hair came into the salon hopefully wielding Pinterest photos showing brilliant, straight locks and how her clients with shining, thin, plaits spent hundreds of dollars on volumizing tonics, perms, and blowouts designed to make their hair look as curly as it would be after a day at the beach. As easy as it would be for her, how strange it would be if every single person was happy leaving the salon with the same exact hairstyle regardless of her personal preference! Imagine trying to get everyone to agree on what style of the afterlife was ideal. *I guess that is the only thing that really makes sense: different Heavens for everyone.*

"You were a hairdresser before you got here?" Patty broke into Jennifer's thoughts. She still had Jennifer's dossier in her lap, and she was reviewing the information that she found in it. Patty patted her voluminous black hair. "Maybe destiny *is* what brought you here! Lord knows I could use some help in the hair department! Norbert, too! Still, it seems kinda strange that a pretty, relatively young lady like yourself would be caught up here in the middle. Let's see if I can get a better picture of what's going on here with you, Sugar…"

Patty scanned through the papers in the dossier more closely. "Oh…I see the problem. Three of your days were *way* too early. Let's see here. June 30, 1992. July 7, 1992. July 14, 1992. Lord above! I wouldn't go to Las Vegas with my retirement money if I was you, Sugar. That is just some *bad luck* to have three of your days fall before you was even a month old. No wonder you didn't do anything good or bad to land you on the light or dark side. Just sitting there eating, sleeping, and blinking while that brain of yours was forming. How on earth is a little thing like that supposed to shape her eternity?"

"My days were too early?"

"Yeah, Baby. Poor thing, too…that's a rough start for sure. Babies bring lots of joy to their worlds just by existing, and they bring lots of heartache, too if they's anything like my son was—that child screamed for the first two years of his life straight. I was ready to take him back to the hospital and see if there was maybe a valve on that voice box of his that they could clamp shut. Then, just like that one morning, a switch went off, and he sat down and had himself a pleasant conversation with me like he'd been reading the newspaper for a few years and finally decided it was time to talk to me about current events…but yes, ma'am, it looks like three of your days were just unlucky early before you even had the chance to say or do anything—never mind doing something exceedingly virtuous."

"But, there's five days. What else does it say. I get two more days, don't I?"

"Yes, Sugar, let's see. Day four: February 12, 2000. It looks like you stayed home sick from school that day with some kind of galloping goo that was going around. It says here that your grandmother came to your house and watched you that morning—"

"I remember that day!" Jennifer remembered that her mom couldn't get off from work and had called her grandmother to come stay at the house and watch her. Usually, Jennifer loved every minute that she got to spend with her grandmother. They would play dress-up with her dolls and make up stories together. But on this particular day, Jennifer could barely muster the strength to get out of bed. She didn't even want to watch *The Price is Right* when her grandmother called her into the living room before lunch. She stayed under her covers, in and out of sleep as the fever coursed through her young body and eventually left the following morning.

"Yes, that day was another dud. Looks like you awoke at 6:26 AM, ate six saltine crackers, finally went to sleep at 10:02 PM and spent most of the day napping in your bedroom. You didn't even kiss your grandmother hello or goodbye that day...and that's not like you. It says here that she's one of your top three people."

She was my only person, Jennifer thought with sadness of her bumpy childhood: the constant fighting between her parents, her father leaving one night and the way the letters slowed up over the years and eventually stopped coming altogether, the numerous moves from cheap place to cheap place, the struggles to focus on school when her home life always seemed to be falling apart. Her grandmother was a bright spot in a childhood that was colored mostly with a lot of bleak gray.

"Lord, Sugar...I have never seen anything like this!" Patty exclaimed as she looked at a final section near the bottom of the sheet of paper containing Jennifer's information. "I'm going to have to check the protocol for what to do in this situation. Looks like your fifth day was also your last day on Earth. There's nothing written here for me to see after 11:59 PM the day before you cashed in those unlucky chips of yours three days ago, Ms. Jennifer."

Cashed in my unlucky chips? "Why can't we see it?"

"It's like I said before, Sugar. No one knows how they die. That last 24 hours is blacked out for everybody. But 'Day Five' is the tie-breaker day for everyone. You had four-neutral days, Sugar. Looks like your last day must have been pretty neutral, too, although I can't be certain because I can't tap in to see what happened on that last day. I can only guess that if it was something bad, you wouldn't be here, and if it was something good, you wouldn't be here either. But, that's water under the bridge like my mama always used to say. Let's go and find Norbert for you. We'll turn this bad luck around, Miss Jennifer. A nice girl like you doesn't belong stuck here, that's for sure."

Chapter 3

"Mr. Norbert, could you please return to your post? Miss Jennifer is waiting for you!" Patty called out into the sterile whiteness.

"Just a minute, Patricia..." Jennifer heard the grumble and muttering of Norbert talking to himself and then the scrape of what she imagined was a cigarette being stamped out by his black oxford shoe. "Just tell her I'll be right there...as if anyone's doing anything other than cooling their heels in this Godforsaken—hello, Darling! I see Madame Patricia of New Orleans has acquainted you with the goings on here in our lovely, little town. That will be all, isn't that right, Miss Patricia? Come on this way, Jennifer."

"You be good to her, Norbert!" Patty chirped, handing him the dossier containing Jennifer's information. "I'll see both of you bright and early tomorrow morning! Don't go scaring this one off on me now, Norbert. She's a good one, and we've got to get her up to the Empire."

Jennifer looked over to see Norbert wincing at the sing-song sound of Patty's cheerful voice. "Ugh...isn't she just the most revoltingly chipper person you've ever encountered? I'd like to know just what's so wonderful about being stuck here in this vacuum like a clothespin spinning around and clogging up the works..." He continued to mutter as they walked together down the long corridor and though glass doors into an office filled with cubicles. "Here we are! *Little House on the Prairie.*"

"This looks like an office." Jennifer took stock of each cubicle along the hallway. There were people of every style and description sitting at desks, reviewing dossiers and files, researching ideas on flowcharts, drawing outlines and making connections between points on maps that lined the cubicle walls. Some spoke languages other than English to people that Jennifer couldn't see. Some tiptoed around the cubicles, appearing to act out a charade or to pantomime a scene to an unknown observer. She watched in amazement as one man fit a missing puzzle piece down into its vacant spot and then proceeded to vanish right before her eyes as if he had never existed in the first place. "What are these people doing? What kind of work do they do here?"

"Well, as Patricia told you, I'm sure…your new position is that of a Revelation 20. That's a bunch of horseshit that means that you've had the misfortune of having a lousy life, and now you get to intervene on the behalf of everyone else who's having a lousy life to make sure that they don't wind up in this boring little hellhole with us. Some people get reincarnated as something else. Some people just go to sleep. Some people have their hearts weighed up against a feather. Us? We're stuck here for now. We're the go-betweens. We're like little gnomes that pop up into the lives of people during their randomly chosen *five* to try to sway their days to good ones so they can reach Empyrea—which is where everyone supposedly wants to go. The Celestial City. The Promised Paradise. Eternity. Call it what you will, Darling, it's the place up top that everyone wants to get to—no matter what they believe, you know what I'm saying?"

Jennifer nodded slowly, taking it all in. "Can you back up to the gnome part?"

"Sure, Darling! I don't really have the same gift of gab as our Resident Guide and dear friend Patricia. Here in the Expiation Zone, we're like little guardian angels to people on the other side, understand? Little Clarences descending down on Bedford Falls to make sure that George Bailey keeps away from bridges, if you know what I mean. Our job is to make sure that the people on our caseloads don't screw up the five lousy days that they have to get to the Empire. We get these little case files, and we zip into the lives of these people to try to make them do something of merit. Something worthy of eternity...not that you could pay me enough to want that for myself, but here we are."

"So, we're guardian angels?"

"Do I look like an angel, darling?" Norbert challenged, pulling a cigarette out from his jacket pocket. There's a lot more between me and Heaven than this rug I've got on my head, let me tell you..."

Jennifer laughed in spite of herself.

"Don't get too proud there, Jennifer. None of us are angels. But we can try to shift the balance so that these people on our caseload might make it up top, see what I'm saying?"

Jennifer was quiet for a moment. She tried desperately to think of the last thing that she remembered doing when she was alive. Patty was right. Her brain did a very good job of completely blacking out the last days of her life. She had no recollection of what she might have done or where she might have been going dressed as she was when she first arrived here in the E.Z. She felt no pain, though, and there was no sadness or worry clouding her thoughts and feelings. In fact, the lightness that she had been experiencing since she arrived was helping her to develop a genuine overall feeling of peace and tranquility in spite of her confusion.

"So...I was 26...when I died?" Jennifer asked finally.

"That's what it says here in the paperwork, Darling. That's awfully young. Were you a smoker?" Norbert asked with genuine interest. "Need a cigarette?" He removed the one that he held in his mouth and held it out to her. She pushed his hand away lightly, waving the smoke away from her face.

"No...no...I never smoked," Jennifer responded, feeling hazy and uncertain again.

"You weren't one of those gals that got around, were you? Is AIDS still a thing down there? I've lost track of current events up here..."

"No! Jeez, Norbert, no...what does it say about me in those papers anyway? No, I didn't sleep around with people. Just the opposite, actually. I stupidly married my high school sweetheart when I was 20 years-old. We went through a divorce last year...I've just been working long hours at the salon to try to keep my head above water and pay off the lawyer, and..."

"You don't suppose he tried to kill you, do you, Jennifer? I've seen that plot played out a thousand times! You know how revolting men can be! They get a whiff of some life insurance or some inheritance money, and then the next thing you know, you're pushing up daisies and he's off in Cabo messing around with anything that moves."

I don't think so. In the absence of the truth, the brain will make up the most elaborate scenes and morph them into a false existence that was never really there, but in this instance, it really was just a sad case of two people who married too young for their own good and decided to call it quits before they lived their whole lives wishing they had done something else.

Although, her ex-husband didn't seem to have much difficulty in moving on.

Twenty-six years…some 'whole life.' Jennifer shook her head in an attempt to rid her mind of the disappointment and sadness that was beginning to take over the peace that she was beginning to feel. Anyway, maybe it was better. Maybe it was better that her life had left her before the inevitable arthritis that befell most hairdressers crept into her hands and feet. Maybe it was better that she never felt the tired mornings of longing to go somewhere—anywhere—and not even being able to walk down the end of the hallway without meeting up with the dull ache of chronic pain. She looked back down at her hands, still young, still capable, and thought how it was better perhaps to have young hands with nothing to hold onto anymore, instead of crepe-covered crooked ones that would cling on forever to something that hurt too much to hold. For the first time since she arrived, she drew a deep breath and decided not to look backward for a while.

"How do you think you died, Norbert?"

"Me? Darling…I spent the better part of 72 years existing on Lucky Strikes, Life Savers, formaldehyde, and jars of applesauce. It's a miracle that I even lived!"

"Good enough," Jennifer agreed. It is the quality of a hairdresser to instantly size up a client and find the common denominator that they share to reveal an initial talking point. So much of human speech had more to do with looking into a mirror and seeing the person inside instead of focusing on the reflection outside. Finding mutual ground was the best way to make it through any service—especially if it was going to be a long one. "Why does this place scare you so badly, Norbert?"

Chapter 4

Most stays in the E.Z. were relatively brief. Though the concept and passing of time does not transfer as neatly to the afterlife as it does to the regimented cycles of life on Earth, for the sake of comparison, after training and initiation, entry-level candidates serve roughly one month making amends and are then characteristically transported north, where they remain in blissful perfection for time indefinite. Being a natural extrovert and people-person, Patricia took a sign-on bonus and chose to stay in middle management at the position of Resident Guide for two years, which would guarantee her a spot in Empyrea, regardless of the success or failure of her expiation. Two years was the longest that anyone stayed in the Expiation Zone in a middle level or executive position. Except for Norbert. Norbert had been in the Expiation Zone for 27 years. In that time, he never desired to move into a middle or executive level position. Despite his initial gray demeanor, he was happily stuck, having neither atoned for nor been castigated to any level worthy of moving upward or downward.

Norbert spent most of the time that he was a Rev. 20 trying to distance himself from whatever initiate was, rather unfortunately, placed in his care so that he could do whatever he wanted and be left alone. None of the initiates ever seemed to take an interest in him, and that was completely fine as far as he was concerned. He wanted nothing more than to hide in his 'office,' away from the business of the work that he was supposed to be doing in the Expiation Zone. "I'm not sure what you mean, Darling," Norbert said quickly, but a slight swiftness to the cadence of his speech betrayed his usually austere demeanor. He coughed quietly into his fist. "Scare? This place doesn't scare me."

"'*This place*'. 'Godforsaken.' 'Hellhole.' 'Little House on the Prairie.' I get the sense that there's someplace you'd rather be, Norbert."

"Oh, on the contrary, Darling. This is *exactly* where I want to be. If I can't go back to my sunny little hideaway in Lauderdale, which, by the way, is not an option, then there's nowhere that I would rather be than where we are right now in the lovely white Expiation Zone. And I *certainly* have no interest in any of the alternatives." Jennifer looked at him quizzically, and he continued. "No one seems to understand my position. Are they still teaching *The Story of Mankind* down there, Jennifer? I've lost a bit of track up here. It's like a boring casino with no clocks, no booze—and no money, for that matter..."

"*The Story of Mankind*? I don't think so. I haven't heard of it. What is it, a movie or something?"

"Well, back when I was in school with the mastodons and sabre-tooth tigers as our class pets, our teachers used to have these books called 'readers.' Right after they were done smacking our sinful little hands with the metal rulers, they would use these giant, thick, nonsensical tomes to indoctrinate us with grammar, arithmetic, and ancient history—of course at that time, ancient history was like the front page headlines of the newspaper, but anyway… I remember Ms. Gultch—I swear—just like right out of *The Wizard of Oz*—Ms. Gultch teaching us about 'The Little Bird of Svithjod' from one of those readers called *The Story of Mankind* or whatever it was."

"I've definitely never heard of that one before," Jennifer said with a laugh.

"No…well, that's probably a good thing. I think they stopped teaching with those 'readers' right around the same time they stopped giving people wooden dentures like the ones George Washington wore." Norbert flashed a winning smile. "I do remember that one story very vividly, though. I can still picture what it looked like in my mind. Let's see…how did it start?…Well, way up in the north country, in this place called Svithjod, there's this giant mountain. The thing's 100 miles high and 100 miles wide."

"Okay, that's, like, unnaturally high, but go on." Jennifer listened with genuine curiosity, wondering if this was just one of Norbert's stories or if there was actually some historical significance to what he was saying.

"Well, once every thousand years, this little bird comes out of wherever it's been hiding, and he sharpens his damn beak against that big, old rock."

"Okay…?" Jennifer wasn't sure where Norbert was going with this story.

"And when that enormous mountain wears away to nothing at all from that noisy, little bird sharpening its beak against it once every thousand years…that's how long it would take for *one day* of eternity to go by."

Jennifer's eyes widened. "That's pretty farfetched, Norbert. They definitely don't teach that story in school anymore. I don't think they have much interest in indoctrinating kids with talk of 'eternity.' I've never heard anything like that. So…the thing that you're afraid of…it's being stuck in the same place forever?"

"Well, let's get something *straight*, Darling. I'm not *afraid* of eternity. I just can't be bothered with it. And I don't especially like birds either. They're noisy. And they're bad luck."

Jennifer decided to leave well-enough alone and see if she could change the subject. *Norbert might be content to stay here, but I'd like to get out sooner than later.* "Well, I'm here now. Maybe your luck with change. Can we get to work?"

Norbert walked Jennifer over to his cubicle, which was at the farthest end of the office. "It goes like this: every morning, you come in and find your paperwork. It'll already be organized and prepared for you each day." He motioned to the mailboxes that were mounted on the wall near his desk. "You won't have your own mailbox yet, so you'll be working along with me—although I use the term 'working' loosely...let's see, here. His arm reached up to the top right corner where Jennifer could see the name 'Berger, Norbert' etched on a small, gold placard beneath the mailbox. Norbert pulled out a manila folder that looked like the one that Patty had containing all of Jennifer's information.

"What poor sap do we have on the docket today?" Norbert glanced through the papers in the small stack. "Adrien Cirillo. Age 32. Day Three. One previous positive. One previous neutral. Chicago, Illinois. Riverwoods Department Police Officer—it's always good to know one of those. Engaged. No children." He closed up the folder with a snap. "Easy as pie..."

"What's 'easy as pie'? What do you do with all of that information?"

"It's like Patricia told you, Darling. Everyone gets five days, and we've got to make them 'righteous' for the sake of the specimens on our caseload. This one's a piece of cake. We've got 24 hours to influence Officer Cirillo to do something of merit today so he can avoid being stuck here in this place with us. He's already got one positive day, which is your ace in the hole, and he's got two more after this one in case you screw up. Basically, as long as he doesn't kill anyone before midnight tonight, we're in the clear. It's almost impossible to botch these things up—try as I might. Although I did accidentally get that one lady embroiled in a murder wrap, but let's just see if we can make this work..."

"How do we make it work? What do we do? Do we, like, spy on him or something."

"Yes and no. In a way, yes...we're influencers. Interveners. These dolts can't hear or see us, and they never know that we're there. Most of 'em still wouldn't notice us if they could these days. Everyone's so wrapped up in themselves that they don't look beyond the ends of their own noses. There's a few rules and restrictions. We can't touch them. We can't talk to them. But we can try to sway them to do something good so that their day gets registered as a positive. That's the name of the game, Darling. Rack up as many positives as you can. It's a win-win, as they say. The saps avoid the E.Z., and you eventually serve your penance and get out of here."

Jennifer nodded her head in understanding, and Norbert continued. "You can drop a penny and have them pick it up, so they whistle while they work and live like it's their lucky day. You can put a certain song on the radio to remind them of their great Uncle Andrew twice removed. You can rearrange their refrigerator pictures so that dear old Dad looks like he's smiling down from Heaven. You can give them a good hair day, so they smile for a change and they're not miserable to their bratty, little kids as they're taking them on an outing to the grocery store. Have them notice the scent of magnolias in the air, get a good seat on the train, get an extra bag of potato chips in the vending machine...get creative, Jennifer! It's your candy store. I usually just like to read their mail and wait until the 24 hours is up, but there are some Rev. 20s who really get their rocks off doing this kind of shit." Norbert reached into his interior jacket pocket and pulled out a cigarette. He put it between his lips and cupped his hands around his mouth to light it. "You ready for this, Darling? It's windy where we're going."

Jennifer opened her mouth to respond, but before any words came out, the white walls of the E.Z. vanished, and she was plunged into cold blackness.

Chapter 5

Jennifer's eyes struggled to focus in the dark that surrounded her. She was still in her black dress and heels, and her arms and legs were immediately met with a chill that she had not felt since before she arrived in the Expiation Zone. "Norbert," she hissed, reaching blindly into the blackness. "Norbert, where are you?" Her searching eyes finally settled on the small orange glow of an ember a few feet away from her. *Norbert's cigarette.* "Norbert, I see you. Where are we?"

"Welcome to your first day, Jennifer," Norbert murmured with a hint of derision as he exhaled the smoke from his cigarette. "We're in Riverwoods, Illinois, a cozy suburb of big-shouldered Chicago, and we have to try to make sure that our specimen, Officer Adrien Cirillo, is a good boy today so we can get out of here and back to the Expiation Zone. I'll be honest with you, though, Darling. I'd rather find someplace warm to hide for the next 24 hours. Lord, I hate when they send me up north to these cold states. I didn't move to Fort Lauderdale for the mosquitos—that's for sure, and these old bones of mine might just shake themselves apart if I catch a chill and start shivering."

The two were on a dark stretch of road on the far outskirts of Chicago. In the blackness of the early morning, a police patrol car cruised slowly along the street, tires slushing against the rain-covered pavement. Tapping his thumbs against the steering wheel, the driver hummed to the beat of Steve Miller Band's "Jet Airliner," which was playing in his head. Adrien Cirillo reached for the Thermos of coffee that was cradled in the console of the cruiser. His black hair was close-cropped, and his small, dark eyes darted watchfully under eyelids that felt heavy from sleep after coming close to the end of his fourth-watch shift. Unbeknownst to Officer Cirillo, Norbert and Jennifer suddenly appeared in the back of the police car. Norbert rubbed his aged hands together and blew into them in an effort to get warm. Jennifer eyed the police officer and her surroundings with interest.

"I take it this is your first time in the back of a police car, Ms. Uccello?" Norbert asked, watching Jennifer's eyes widen. He took a break from rubbing his hands together and opted instead for a cigarette, his preferred method for warming up.

"Oh, definitely," Jennifer responded, peering at the numerous buttons, computer screens, and radio controls that made this car differ from most of the vehicles she'd been in. "How about you?" She turned to him. Norbert was still a mystery to her. His seeming disdain for everything and everyone might have soured most people, but there was something in his eyes and his demeanor that put Jennifer at ease and made her want to break down the wall that he had constructed around himself.

"Well, believe it or not, I used to know my way around a lot of cars—police ones included," Norbert said, taking a drag on his cigarette and exhaling the smoke away from Jennifer. "That was back in the good old days when you could still fix a car with a screwdriver and a pair of pliers, but I digress. Anyway, cops love a funeral, and I've lined up more vehicles for processions than Ford has cued up on an assembly line. 'Course, if we're talking cars, I'd take a nice Lincoln or Cadillac hearse over a Crown Victoria any day of the week."

"Why would anyone want to drive a hearse?" Jennifer asked, casually waving the smoke away from her face.

"Oh, I had a whole fleet of them, Darling! I was in the funeral business," Norbert stamped out his cigarette between his fingers and flashed a Cheshire cat smile. "Death suits me."

"Yeesh..." Jennifer couldn't tell if he was kidding or not, but she continued on. "You know, I almost took a job with a funeral home when I first graduated from beauty school. There was a sign-on bonus and everything," she said, exhibiting her skill as a hairdresser by trying to make the best of the awkward silence that sometimes took over a conversation—even one as strange as this.

"Well, you made the right choice in dealing with the living, Darling. There's no worse tipper than a cadaver—especially if you forget to clamp the brake down on the lift system when you're lowering it down into the casket..." Jennifer's eyes widened in initial shock, but she looked over at Norbert and was relieved to see that the twinkle in his green eyes indicated that this was just his kidding dry and dark sense of humor driving the conversation. "Sorry...corpse humor..."

She laughed uncomfortably. "So...why did you become a funeral director—besides the Cadillacs?" she finally asked after a moment as Officer Cirillo passed a small cemetery and continued to smoothly navigate the cruiser through the dark streets of Riverwoods, stopping at each intersection and inspecting each area carefully as he drove on.

"It was a family business," Norbert quipped, taking a long drag from his cigarette. "I inherited it from my old man. Now, there was someone who was a perfect candidate for dealing with people who didn't have a pulse anymore." He took another drag and exhaled. "You know, he was so cold and heartless when he was alive, it took three doctors to sign off on the death certificate to prove that the old bastard was finally dead when he eventually bit the dust. We'd have kept him around, frowning in his armchair, for another week or two, unable to tell the difference."

Jennifer smirked. Sometimes, she wasn't sure if she could believe half of the things that came out of Norbert's mouth. "We thought about installing one of those bells on the coffin," Norbert continued. "You know the ones that they used when everyone caught cholera in the 1700s for the corpse to ring if it accidentally got buried alive. 'Course, that's old grouch probably wouldn't have rung the bell to save his miserable soul if he were still kicking in there—he hated the sound of music so much."

"Norbert, you're too much—" Jennifer was about to go on, but the police car suddenly came to an unexpected stop.

"Oooh," Norbert crooned softly, stretching his neck to try to get a better view of the scene. Jennifer's thin brows knit together in concern as she watched Officer Cirillo press a button, which caused the lights of the patrol car to flash brightly in the darkness of the still-sleeping dawn. "What have we here?" Norbert purred. Adrien took a breath, deftly patted his side where his weapon was fixed to his belt, and self-assuredly opened the door of the cruiser into the uncertainty of the blackness.

Officer Adrien Cirillo's ten-year career had not turned out the way that he wanted it to. He grew up in the heart of Chicago, and his father was the First Deputy Superintendent of Police for Chicago's main precinct. He had loved everything about crime fighting since he could remember, and he knew that he wanted to be a police officer just like his father when he grew up. Adrien was a star member of the academy and hoped to follow in his father's footsteps when he graduated. Unfortunately, what he thought was a relatively innocuous and accidental injury to his left eye that he had sustained early on in his career forced him to be passed over for one of the Chicago positions, and he was relegated to a mundane post in the outskirts of the city in the Riverwoods Police Force, where he had remained as a sheriff up until this point. Over the course of ten years, he hadn't seen as much excitement in his whole career as he used to see in one day on the job when he was still working downtown. Still, each day presented an opportunity for fortune to display itself anew. Adrien self-assuredly headed in the direction of something that caught his interest in a wooded area off the side of the road and out of reach of the dim streetlights that glowed hazy in the cool early morning. What he lacked in vision, he made up for in keen intuition, and he often sensed that something was wrong much before his eagle-eyed peers could even see it.

Jennifer and Norbert squinted from the backseat and then quickly appeared outside the patrol car behind Officer Cirillo so that they could try to see what he was sensing in the impenetrable dark. Adrenaline began to pump through all three. Maybe in an hour, the rosy light of dawn would begin to illuminate the strange scene that was unfolding before them: a giant, heavy antique car, leaking fluid with its white-walled back wheels suspended in midair as it teetered precariously in the bushes, its nose pointing downward toward a steep ravine. But at this time of the dark night, on the outskirts of Chicago, only the alternating red and blue of the flashing police lights betrayed the blackness that surrounded them.

Chapter 6

"Norbert?" Jennifer called with both fear and excitement. "Can you see anything?"

"Darling, these eyes couldn't see a damned thing before I died twenty-seven years ago," Norbert grumbled as he reached into his jacket pocket for his reading glasses, which he kept next to his cigarettes. "Let's see," he said, placing them on the end of his nose. "Nope. Not a damned thing…"

Officer Cirillo took in a long breath. There was something in the air that was not germane to the usual Riverwoods night, but he couldn't make out what it was. He shone his flashlight along the edge of the mature shrubbery that dotted the roadside. Jennifer walked closer to where the light was shining. From the road, it looked as if there was an intentional break in the bushes that edged the berm of the road. She squinted and walked closer toward it. Immediately, she filled with excitement and fear. "Nobert! Come quick! This must be a car accident! I think there's someone trapped in here!"

"Well, wouldn't that be just our luck," Norbert muttered under his breath, feigning disinterest as he secretly filled with an emotion that he hadn't felt in decades. This was the first time in years that he had actually gotten close in proximity to one of the subjects on his case load. On any other given day, he would have warmly waited in the back of the police cruiser, peering nosily out the window, smoking cigarettes, and enjoying the ride around town without doing anything to sway the course of the day to positive. Since he had become a Rev. 20, he found that, though Dante Alighieri had said that the darkest places in hell were reserved for those who maintained neutrality, noninterference was exactly what Norbert chose to uphold. He avoided working to get positives. If he earned one at all, it was by complete accident. Much to his dismay, it seemed that good fortune orbited Officer Cirillo and Jennifer this dark morning. He might get a 'positive' tally without any intersession or meddling whatsoever.

Jennifer walked past the bushes and toward the scene. Nothing could have prepared her for what she would find as she walked closer. An antique white and pink car with a heavy chrome bumper and giant, fin-shaped taillights appeared to be suspended in midair as it dove toward a cliff. Inside, a shocked and unconscious elderly woman named Irma Larsen, dressed only in a floral nightgown and wearing purple curlers in her white hair, was held against the wheel of the precariously teetering car as a swarm of cats mingled and meowed around her.

"What the—?" Jennifer had never seen anything like it.

"Oooh," Norbert hummed with interest as he appeared next to Jennifer, not paying nearly as much attention to the endangered woman pinned inside as he did to the car itself. "I haven't seen one of these in years. 1956 Buick Century Convertible. Folding roof. Eight cylinders. Power windows. Power steering. Automatic transmission…no seatbelts," he added, looking suddenly with a shade of worry at the trapped Mrs. Larsen.

"Does it have a radio?" Jennifer asked quickly, keenly remembering Norbert's words to her when he was first reviewing the role of the Revelation 20: *You can put a certain song on the radio to remind them of their great Uncle Andrew twice removed.*

"Right above the cigarette lighter and the ashtray," Norbert reminisced fondly.

Jennifer carefully reached over the passenger side and gingerly brushed against a cat sitting on the white leather seat. Feeling the cool spirit nearby, the cat let out a menacing shriek, which immediately caught the attention of Officer Cirillo some 50 yards away. He began advancing in the darkness toward the scene, and Jennifer hurriedly pushed a button on the dashboard and turned it up as loud as she could. The crackling speakers whirred to life, and Steve Miller's voice sang into the silence of the night, *"But my heart keeps calling me backwards as I get on the 707…"*

Officer Cirillo broke into a run and pushed his way through the dense shrubbery that surrounded the car. Surveying the scene quickly, he called for backup on his radio as he flung open the door. The rush of cold air immediately revived the unconscious Mrs. Larsen. "Trudy!" she called out hoarsely to one of her cats, who had hastily jumped out of the door.

"Ma'am, are you alright?" Officer Cirillo carefully put his arms around the frail woman, but she gripped the steering wheel tightly.

"My cats," she uttered, uncertainly. She was still discombobulated by the events of the evening. She had awoken from a dream and had gone out into the garage to look for one of her cats, Tootsie, thinking that it was time to give it its medicine. In doing so, she had left the door that led from the kitchen to the garage open for the five other cats that she meticulously kept as pets to pass through. While she was in the car searching for Tootsie, she forgot what she was doing and assumed that she must have been going to the store. She turned the key in the ignition of her Buick and slowly backed out into the darkness, but she was unaccustomed to driving at night, and she soon became disoriented. The blackness, her own tiredness, the six cats, and a rather large deer, which she mercifully swerved to avoid, eventually got the better of her. Her car veered off the road, and the colossal Buick was now caught on some branches, which kept it from plummeting into Des Plaines River on the edge of town.

"I'll get your cats for you," Adrien assured her calmly. "I need you to come with me, Ma'am. Will you let me help you?" There was something in the deep, dark eyes that Mrs. Larsen trusted. She allowed him to wrap his arms around her and carefully pull her from the driver's side of the car. With her came two cats. In the distance, the sound of sirens blared as flashing lights worked in tandem with the approaching dawn to shed light on the strange scene that outspread on the Illinois morning. As Officer Cirillo began carefully picking up addled cats and placing them, purring, near the disoriented Mrs. Irma Larsen, two other police officers ran toward the scene. They attached a tow rope to the car and were able to pull it to safety as the radio continued blaring into the emerging dawn, *"Don't carry me too far away. Oh, big ole jet airliner, cause it's here that I've got to stay…"*

"Careful with that bumper," Norbert grumbled, unheard and unheeded, to one of the other attending police officers, who was radioing information back to the barracks as he walked around the vehicle. "You'll have a hell of a time coming up with enough chrome to replace one like that these days."

Jennifer was filled with relief and pride. This was her first day, and it seemed like it was a successful mission. Adrien Cirillo had saved Mrs. Irma Larsen—and all six of her cats—from a whole slew of certain disasters that would have befallen them if he had not found them in time and came to their rescue. "I think we did it, Norbert," she said slowly as she looked over to where Mrs. Larsen was wrapped in a blanket, holding two cats in her arms and scratching them behind the ears.

"Well, that's as may be," Norbert grumbled. "Thank God it wasn't one of that old Buick's five days," he said, eyeing where the dainty side-view mirrors hung grotesquely from their once prominent spot near the curve of the windshield. "I don't think there's anyone left on Earth who knows how to fix the undercarriage of an old beaut' like that anymore. Christ, those things looked like jungle gyms and were twice as filled with tetanus. That poor old boat's never going to sail again. They'll probably just tow it off to the junkyard. I guess I still have a lot to teach you." Through Norbert's apparent disappointment in the fate of the Buick, a genuine smile formed on the thin line of his lips.

Jennifer smiled in spite of Norbert's mock ridicule. As the sun lifted itself high in the morning sky, she felt a rising sensation in herself. Day was finally here. And it was a good one.

Chapter 7

"How come no one ever talks about God up here, Norbert? I've been here for three days now, and outside of what Patty said about the 'book of life' in her initial greeting, I haven't heard anything about God or religion," Jennifer said, her brow furrowed.

"And you won't hear anything about it from me either, Darling. Let's not get too excited by yesterday's events, lest we forget the main credos of the Revelation 20s: don't handle the specimens, don't say anything to them, and—one that I've added for my own well-being—don't cloud the impressionable young cadets' minds with talk of God…and all for the same reason. Most of the saps down there on Earth can't see beyond the ends of their noses long enough to notice that we're even around them, and the dead folks up here in the E.Z. are the exact same way. When it comes to God, all most people can think about is what's in it for them—whether they're alive or not."

There really wasn't much argument with that notion, Jennifer thought. Still, she had some unanswered questions, and she was on a bit of a high after her first successful day in training as a Rev. 20. She was disappointed that Norbert, with his 27 years of experience, wouldn't share even a grain of information with her on the subject.

Norbert picked up on her curiosity. "Did I ever tell you about Phil? Phil DePrimo from Devine's Vault, Urn, and Monument Company?"

"No, Norbert…You still have a lot to teach me, remember?"

"Well, Phil was my main contact for the needs of the bereaved," Norbert began in his lofty way. His green eyes began to twinkle in remembrance. "No one could upsell a casket like old Phil. If you ordered 'Basic,' suddenly, you'd be hearing the virtues of the 'Basic Plus.' If dear Aunt Tilly always dreamed of being visited and viewed in the 'Premium Package,' old Phil would have her laid out in the 'Luxury Limitless' line—complete with a headstone you could build a two-car garage on top of. I stayed in the funeral business for the cars and the clothes. Phil stayed in it for the accessories—always trying to entice people to reach for the next level. Each new season, I'd get a catalog containing all the literature on what 'the deceased of today' needed—you know how trendy these stiffs like to be when they're resting in peace, right?"

Jennifer laughed in spite of herself.

"But, Phil was fair—and you couldn't beat the craftsmanship and quality you received from Devine's Vault, Urn and Monument. You know, fifteen years went by, and I never once met face-to-face with Phil. I'd call on a Monday, and we'd shoot the breeze a while. I'd mail the checks out on a Wednesday, receive a fruitcake in the mail every Christmas. Devine's delivery people were always on time, friendly, and accommodating. Phil was reliable. Things were different, then, before the 'web' or whatever-the-hell you call it. A lot of stuff was done by mail and phone, and we just stayed with people we'd known for years. My father had always used Devine's, and I just went along with what he did after he left the business to me. I was completely lost when I first took over, and Phil guided me in the right direction on a lot of things.

"Since I was indebted for the kindness, old Phil and I shared a lovely, dependable business relationship over the years. Well, one Monday I called up Phil at Devine's to place my weekly order, and a new person picked up the phone. I had to recheck my Rolodex to make sure I had the extension right and said, 'I'd like to speak with Phil, please,' and damned if the lady who answered the phone didn't tell me that Phil had passed away just that morning! Jeez Louise, I felt like a part of me had died! Well, I wanted to go and honor Phil for all the business that we did together over the years and all the help I got in the beginning when I first took the funeral parlor over. Christ, I had a devil of a time finding out the funeral arrangements because Devine's Vault, Urn, and Monument was located clear across the state in Naples, and there was no easy way of looking up people's addresses back then like there is now, but I figured that I owed it to old Phil to pay my respects…plus, I wanted to see if that old churl went all out and decided to be buried in the top shelf collection or if he was just going to be laid out in a cardboard box and buried in a groundhog burrow in his own backyard."

Jennifer covered her mouth to hide the smile that was forming as she listened to Norbert recount the story.

"Well, I was sweating like a pig from three hours in that old Lincoln, studying a map of the great state of Florida while dodging rogue crocodiles in the Goddamned Everglades, when I pulled up to the corpse house. I remember thinking, 'This must be the place' because there were about 50 other hearses crammed in the parking lot of that funeral parlor. If you want a good time, go to a mortician's wake—or anyone associated with the entombment business, really. You'd be hard-pressed to find more bullshit if you were mucking out stalls at a rodeo. Everyone is as sympathetic and 'sorry-for-your-loss' as hell. Well, I stood in that line for about two hours waiting to pay my last respects to Phil, and the strangest thing happened. I thought I was in the wrong place the closer I got to the casket. The pictures they had exhibited for Phil were of a blonde woman, and the flower arrangements all spoke of Phil as being a dear 'Wife,' 'Aunt,' and 'Mother'. I picked up a prayer card from the table when I finally got close enough, and I realized that Phil DePrimo, my head contact, whom I'd known and conversed with on the phone on a weekly basis for fifteen straight years, was none other than Mrs. Phyllis Joan DePrimo-Firmstone, owner and operator of Devine's Vault, Urn, and Monument Company!"

Jennifer laughed. "You've got to be kidding me, Norbert! You couldn't tell over the phone that you were speaking to a woman instead of a man for fifteen years?"

"Old Phil had an octave range somewhere between a bullfrog and Bea Arthur, Jennifer. Her voice would have been deep even for a man's! That poor woman must have single-handedly paid for the college tuitions of all of the Philip Morris great-grandchildren. Christ, and I thought I was bad. I've seen briskets with less smoke damage on them than that woman had—and that's after the undertakers smeared makeup on her like they were frosting a cake." Norbert shook his head. "Lord, did that throw me for a loop... 'Phil' was short for 'Phyllis' this whole time, and I never even knew it."

Jennifer looked at Norbert as he stared, still so lost in the moment, it was as if he were transported back to that funeral home three hours away from his hometown, smelling the roses and gardenias and lilies left in sympathy and remembrance for Mrs. Phyllis DePrimo-Firmstone of Naples,

Florida, the female proprietor of Devine's Vault, Urn, and Monument, who had chosen to be laid out in the Platinum Jacqueline line with a tufted lilac satin interior and a custom engraved, polished granite headstone in the shape of a heart. "Norbert...?" Jennifer asked after a moment or two.

Norbert stirred suddenly away from the familiar scents and sounds and back to the sterile reality of the E.Z. "Norbert," she squinted at him, seeing a change and wondering if he was feeling alright. "Are you feeling okay?"

"I'm fine, Jennifer," Norbert said dryly, back to his old self. "I spent most of my life completely happy with who I thought Phil DePrimo was, and I was just shocked at the time to find out that old Phil wasn't anything like what I had guessed him to be. You know what's funny? I really liked Phil, but I think I would have liked *Phyllis* even more if I had gotten to know her better. She was a wife, aunt, mother...all the things I never really had in my life. No wonder we got on so well. After the wake and at the post funeral luncheon, I got to talking to her relatives and a few people who worked with her. Like me, she inherited her business from her father...but she did real well at it. She was the best there was, Jennifer. Once she died and Devine's changed hands, it just wasn't the same without her. I wound up going to some other guy a few towns over, and it was just business as usual once Phil wasn't there anymore. Even if I had her all wrong, my business was truly a lot better with Phil—Phyllis—than without. Phil wasn't what I expected, but it doesn't take away from how good things were when we worked together. I didn't know it at the time, but I was dealing with someone even better than I could have thought, and here I just wasted my Mondays in meaningless conversation and my Wednesdays sending over checks without ever getting to know anything about Devine's or who was running the show. I guess that's the way it goes."

Jennifer looked, still concerned at Norbert. There was something in his face that she didn't know well enough to place, and she assumed he might just be homesick with all the talk of Florida and the funeral business.

She didn't know that he was shaken because, in sharing his story of Phil, he had broken two rules of his own personal Revelation 20 creed that he had developed over 27 years of chosen isolation and introversion: don't get too close to the cadets. And don't talk about God.

Chapter 8

"Well, aren't you two getting along just fine?" Patty crowed as she neared Norbert's cubicle while making her rounds of the office section of the E.Z. with a clipboard in her hand. "Norbert, this one's a keeper! You done snagged yourself a tally in the 'plus' column with Officer Cirillo saving that nice old lady, Mrs. Larsen. You, too, Miss Jennifer. That's a step in the right direction, for sure. I bet you can almost taste the gumbo and andouille sausage they's cooking up for you in that Empire in the sky!"

"Good morning, Patricia," Norbert purred. "That's "Norbert B-E-R-G-E-R if you're planning, in your Resident Guide greatness, on ordering me a plaque for 'Employee of the Month.' I wouldn't want any Freudian slips in case you're getting a little lunch hungry—what with all the hard work you do around here, dreaming of the dinner you're going to have when you finally get that promotion you've been gunning for."

"Well, you can say what you like, Mr. Norbert *Berger*, but I am very proud of you! That's the first positive you've gotten since I've been here— and probably for years before that! And I think you need to give Miss Jennifer a little credit where credit is due." Patricia looked at Jennifer, sized her up, and smiled. "I knew you were going to be a natural the minute you arrived here! You're a real go-getter, Baby. Playing that song like that so Officer Cirillo could hear where that car was! Now, keep that fire blazing! Line up those dominoes, and knock 'em down. You're one step closer to the door already."

Norbert's eyes rolled deep into the back of his head, and Jennifer smirked at him and smiled genuinely at Patty. "Thanks, Patty. Maybe it was just beginner's luck," she shrugged.

"There were six black cats in that Buick in Illinois, Jennifer. I'm pretty sure 'luck' had nothing to do with it," Norbert grumbled, lighting up a cigarette, taking a long drag, and then deliberately blowing the smoke away from Jennifer and out of the corner of his mouth toward Patricia. "Where are we off to today, O great and powerful Resident Guide? Could you be a dear and grab that case file out of my mailbox please?"

Patty coughed and waved her arm to dissipate the smoke that Norbert had blown toward her and reached up into his mailbox to retrieve the dossier. "Here you go, Norbert," she said, handing the manila folder to him. "You know, we're switching over to an electronic system soon. They're going to be phasing out the paper folders and dossiers, and you'll have an electronic tablet with all the caseload information programmed right on it to help streamline the process. Everything will be kept in the cloud—ain't that funny, Norbert? They call it 'The Cloud.' I'll be doing the training for the rollout in the next few weeks."

"Is that right?" Norbert purred, disinterested as he took a long drag on his cigarette. "Well, you and your cloud can just send some smoke signals up over to my office when you're ready, and I'll respond back with a few puffs at my earliest convenience." Once again, he blew the smoke in Patty's direction, and she began to walk away, waving her hands in the air in an effort to dispel the smoke.

"I don't know what I'm gonna do with that man and those stogies of his, driving me crazy with that ever-loving—" she stopped midsentence as if she suddenly remembered herself and turned around to face the two of them. "Jennifer—" she maintained, looking intently with her own fierce eyes into the timid, brown eyes of the new initiate, "you keep up the good work. That was a fine performance that you turned in, in Illinois, and I think that those 'neutrals' you had all through your life are not at all indicative of the kind of person that you are. No, ma'am, you are anything but neutral. Like I said, you're a natural, Miss Jennifer. And you keep Mr. Norbert in line—which is no easy task, that's for darn sure."

Jennifer smiled at Patty and then walked closer to Norbert's desk. He had haphazardly thrown the contents of the folder onto his desk and was tilting himself back on his chair enjoying the last of his cigarette. "Who have we got today, Norbert?"

"This one's not exactly in either of our wheelhouses, Darling," Norbert began. "Casie Gale. Age 33. Day Four. One previous negative. One previous positive. One previous neutral. Sleepy little town of Nazareth, Pennsylvania. Married. Stay-at-home-mother to three children. *Ick...*"

"'Ick' to the three kids, being a stay-at-home-mom, being 'married,' or living in Nazareth, Pennsylvania?" Jennifer wondered, grabbing the dossier and flipping through it with a concerned look on her face. "What is it about *this* one that you don't like?"

"'It's all pretty icky here, Darling. You've got a two and a seven in this hand, and none of the suits match up. This gal is on her fourth day with one tally in each slot, and there's not enough time in the day of a mother of three to run a comb through her hair and brush her teeth—never mind to do something of merit. When someone like this shows up on my caseload, I usually just hide in the corner away from all the screaming, flying Cheerios, and spaghetti stains and watch the clock, waiting in earnest for my day to be over."

"Well, we can't do that today, Norbert," Jennifer said with finality. "Today is going to be a great day. A *positive* day," she persisted, trying to convince herself. "Let's get going!" She returned all of the pages from the case file back to the dossier and tapped the edges on the desk so that everything fit together with flush precision. "Time's wasting."

Norbert rolled his eyes, took a cigarette out of his jacket pocket and placed it between the thin line of his lips. "Suit yourself," he said without taking the cigarette out of his mouth and lighting up. "Let's see if the town of Nazareth can stir up yet another miracle."

Chapter 9

"Mama? Mama? MAMA!" a towheaded boy screamed as he pulled on the hem of Casie Gale's t-shirt. "Mama, I need a fresh diaper."

"You're not wearing a diaper—oh, shoot—Jackson!" she rubbed a hand down her face in an effort to clear her mind and mentally counted to four while exhaling deeply. "Jackson, honey…" she lowered herself to his level and looked into his wide, gray eyes. "When you feel like you have to go potty, you—"

"Mom! Landon's biting me!" another boy, this one about five, called from the other room.

"I feel like I have to tap out here, Jennifer," Norbert remarked as soon as he appeared in the dining room amid the toys, stray puzzle pieces, goldfish crackers, and Legos that were strewn about the entirety of the Gale house. "I'll see you in 24 hours…"

"Not so fast, Norbert," Jennifer said, staying Norbert by gently grabbing the arm of his jacket. It looks like Casie Gale needs all the help she can get here."

Jennifer watched as Casie cleaned up the mess that Jackson's failed attempt at potty training had left on the ground, popped a binkie into the mouth of little Landon, and then handed the oldest a newly opened can of Pringles with one deft movement and all without blinking an eye. She went around tidying the house while the three small boys seemed to get into new messes just as quickly. Despite the outward appearance of chaos, there was an air of confidence and genuine contentment to Casie. After seeing that the five-year-old was settled with his snack in front of the TV and that Jackson was busy putting together a puzzle, Casie finally sat down at the kitchen island and began to assemble what appeared to be suction cups, bottles, and tubing and brought them close to her chest.

"What the hell is going on here, Jennifer?" Norbert asked, turning away from the scene.

"She's pumping, Norbert," Jennifer explained with a hint of loss of patience. "She pumping milk to feed her little baby."

"I think this is my cue to exit," Norbert continued walking away. "I'll be in the den watching Captain Kangaroo if you need me. 'Pumping milk,' for crying out loud...now I've seen everything."

Jennifer took a deep breath. "I get it, Norbert. This is uncomfortable, but we still have to help her." Jennifer slowly surveyed the room. She couldn't talk to or touch Casie, but she had free reign of anything else in the house to use to her advantage, and there was no shortage of stuff in the Gale house. She eyed the piles of stuffed animals, matchbox cars, dinosaur puppets, action figurines, books, and clean but unfolded laundry that carpeted the house. *No help there.* She stepped closer to Casie and peered over her shoulder to see what she was looking at on her phone. *'Moms and Milk Support Group'* she read aloud as she looked at the heading of the group at the top of Casie's phone's screen. She watched as Casie scrolled through posts containing questions on pumping schedules and quickly entered comments and answers to queries and questions that she encountered as she came upon them on the feed. Jennifer suddenly filled with hope and excitement. "Norbert! Norbert, get over here! Casie's a group moderator! She runs a breastfeeding blog!"

"Are those English words you're saying, Jennifer? You're not really making much sense to me, Darling. And I'll stay right here until old Bessy puts those udders away and moves on out to pasture, thank you very much."

Jennifer sighed deeply. She was the initiate, but this was a case in which she would have to teach her mentor if there was any hope of getting a 'positive' for the day. "Norbert, I know you don't like any of this 'newfangled' stuff, but there's this thing called 'the internet.' It's like…a very large electronic newspaper with all the information you could ever need on it."

"Oh, I've heard of all that hocus pocus, Darling…I just don't have much use for it—"

"Yes, you do!" Jennifer insisted. "Casie fields questions on this board for moms looking for information about feeding their babies. It's a support group."

"I'm listening…" Norbert purred.

"She might save a baby's life today just by answering a question! It's almost a guaranteed 'positive'! We're in the clear!"

"Mmmmnnnnnn. No. Too easy, Darling. I've seen this a few times when I've had some other Millennials pass through as cadets. You guys are still wired to your phones, and you think it can do everything for you in the E.Z. like it did for you on Earth. It doesn't work that way, Jennifer. That's just not the way it happens if you want to earn your day. You can't poke a few buttons on the phone and get a medal of honor badge and a ticket to the Empire that way, Sweetie. There's nothing righteous enough in a phone that'll get you and her over to the other side."

Jennifer looked again, defeatedly, around the house. Something told her that the support group was a long shot, but it was all she had. From her vantage point behind Casie, she could see all the queries in threads. Most of them were relatively straight-forward. There were questions on which bottles to use, how long to nurse, which pumps yielded the highest output. *'It's your candy store,' Norbert had said at the beginning.* Thinking quickly, Jennifer used what little power and insight she had as a Rev. 20 to review the contents of the blog and to go through the older pages of the board that Casie had missed while getting her three children ready to start the day. Most of the posts were mundane, but one caught her attention.

"Not really nursing related…just need to vent." With her interest piqued, Jennifer began to read through the post, which seemed to have gotten lost in the shuffle of the numerous other posts about positioning, lip ties, and latching.

Long post ahead, sorry in advance. I am feeling so bittersweet right now, the post began. *It's been four years since I lost my son. He was born at 35 weeks gestation, and he passed away before he was delivered as a result of complications with my placenta. I was rushed into the hospital quickly and unexpectedly because my water had broken. When I first arrived and they hooked me up to the machines, I heard his beautiful heartbeat and was filled with hope, but in spite of all that the doctors tried to do to save him, my son's heartbeat dropped too low to sustain him. I watched the equipment that showed his glimmer of a heartbeat slow and come to a final stop. The doctors and nurses worked quickly, but there was just no saving my sweet, little boy. After I delivered him, the doctors said that my husband and I could stay in the room with him for as long as we needed. I needed forever. I needed the lifetime that was taken from him—from me. At the same time, I wanted to run...but to run backward into yesterday, to a time when everything was as it should be and hope still filled my body instead of so much sadness. My husband and I were so caught up in all the grief of what we were feeling in those first couple weeks after we lost him that we were just sort of going through the motions on auto-pilot.*

A knot began to form in Jennifer's throat as she continued to read through the post with glassy eyes.

We made the funeral arrangements, and we decided that he would be buried in what was supposed to be his coming-home outfit. At the time, I was furious at my husband because he took a picture of him lying there in his little casket. I didn't think that taking pictures of him like that was a good idea. I wanted to take pictures of him blowing out his birthday candles, playing with salamanders, and learning to crawl. I wanted pictures of my son enjoying life—not being so tiny with his life taken from him. Now, years later…I'm happy that I at least have one picture to remember him by. It's been four years, and this picture is all I have of him.

I do have some good news to share. I'm happy to say that I recently gave birth to a sweet little girl named Molly. She is strong and gentle. Sometimes, when I am nursing her, she nods off to sleep, and in her peaceful lips, I see the beautiful, perfect red lips of her brother. Sometimes, I think God gave her lips like my son so that I can see his smile each time I see hers—and I hope there are many, many opportunities to do that. I just wish that there was something I could give her of her older brother. While I am so happy to hold and love my daughter, I sometimes feel overcome by the loss of my son and the feeling that she'll (and I'll) never know her big brother. I wish there was something that I could actually hold onto of his. They don't even make pajamas that look like this anymore. This picture and Molly's smile are all I have. Thanks for listening. Dana.

Jennifer's wiped the tears that were streaming silently down her face. The feed on Casie's phone appeared blurry through her own tears, but on it she could make out the attached image of a small, sweet boy, eyes closed in peaceful sleep. She looked at his delicate, perfect hands and his red, heart-shaped lips. Despite her sadness, she smiled at the playful pastel dinosaurs that romped along the pajamas of what was supposed to be this sweet boy's going-home outfit.

Wait a minute. Jennifer's eyes left the screen of the phone and quickly perused the floor of the Gale house. There was something in the spirited pattern of the little boy's pajamas that looked strikingly familiar. Her gaze fell on the sleeve of some pajama bottoms that were inching their way out from under the laundry basket. Jennifer looked from the phone to the pile and back to the phone again. "Norbert!" she called. "Norbert, come look at this!"

"I think I've seen enough for today, Darling," Norbert groaned from the other room.

"No, I mean it! Come here!"

Chapter 10

Norbert reluctantly walked over to where Jennifer was positioned behind Casie's back, and Jennifer excitedly pointed from the screen of Casie's phone to the pile of laundry on the floor. "See!" She filled him in on the story of the original post. "Casie hasn't seen this post yet, but I was able to go through the old threads on the page and find it. I think we may have a way to turn today into a positive. I just need to make sure that she sees this post and that laundry!"

While Norbert was certainly no expert in the field of technology or network engineering, years of working as a funeral director had given him a certain level of experience and understanding that he often wished he didn't possess. He recognized the depth of what he was looking at in the picture before Jennifer had even said anything to him about its background, and somewhere in the part of his heart that he had trained to silence, an ache took root.

"I think you're onto something here, Jennifer," Norbert marveled huskily, hiding the catch in his throat with one of his characteristic coughs. "Let me be on cleanup detail. You work that hoodoo machine."

Jennifer pushed a few buttons and brought the post to the forefront of Casie's phone screen and then watched Casie's eyes focus on what she was reading. She initially scrolled down quickly and almost deleted the post when she saw that it wasn't related to breastfeeding, but she then retraced her finger and continued to read from the top. Jennifer watched as Casie's gray eyes turned wet and sorrow knit itself into the light brows of the tired mom of three. Overcome with emotion, Casie tearful gaze fell to where her own children were sitting in the living room. To say that they were a handful was an understatement, but as she looked at her youngest's innocent blue eyes, the bright yellow mop of her middle son's hair, and the perfect smile that curved over the lips of her oldest as he watched a tyrannosaurus roar on the TV set, she felt so grateful for the bedlam that filled her life as a mom—suddenly her eyes settled on something on the floor of the living room.

Part of her survival as a mother of three hinged on her ability to almost obliviously ignore the messes that seemed to grow like weeds around her house, but there was an aspect of her surroundings that registered in her mind immediately at that moment. Splayed out directly beneath Landon, where Norbert had keenly placed it, was a pair of pajamas printed with frolicking pastel dinosaurs. These pajamas had belonged to her oldest son when he was a baby, and she had just washed them after taking them out of storage to see if they would fit Landon. Casie's eyes studied the screen. She unhooked the suction cups from the pump, put the parts in soapy water in the sink, put the milk-filled bottles in the refrigerator, and then walked over to where her boys were sitting. An idea crept into her head, and she feverishly responded to the original post.

Dear Dana. Thank you so much for sharing your story. Can you please DM me your mailing address? I think that I can help you to share a part of your son with your daughter Molly.

Casie had embraced motherhood with fervor. Although she had gone back to work six weeks after her oldest was born, she threw herself headlong into being the kind of mom who did everything for her children. She traded her job in fashion marketing for that of full-time stay-at-home mom when her second son, Jackson, had been born, and with the arrival of Landon, she knew that she was there to stay. To maintain her connection to the outside world, she wrote blogs about breastfeeding and moderated a support group. She tried her hand at cloth diapering and authoritative parenting. With her first son, she made her own purees and baby foods. She even attempted making crafts with him. In her research on crafting with babies, she came upon a pattern of how to make teddy bears out of outgrown baby clothes to use as keepsakes for children. Eventually, Jackson arrived, and she didn't have much time for crafting anymore and never got around to using the pattern. Still, she knowingly picked up the dinosaur pajamas as a smile spread over her face. While the boys played, she spent part of that morning putting her fashion sense to good use in creating the stuffing for and then cutting and sewing the fabric of what would become an adorable teddy bear—for just the right recipient.

The boys looked on with curiosity at what their mom was doing. Twice, Casie had to stop Jackson, who kept trying to take the unfinished bear away, but she explained that the pajamas used to belong to his older brother, and that the teddy bear was going to a new home—with a little sister. The mere mention of a "little sister" was enough to sour Jackson and make him move onto something more exciting, and though most days went by in a whirlwind at the Gale house, the boys were unexpectedly agreeable to one another on this particular day. The older ones colored quietly, and little Landon napped for much longer than he typically did most days. Maybe it was the quiet buzz of Norbert's constant and unusual hum that helped him sleep a bit longer that morning than he normally did.

By lunchtime, Casie had completed her project, and she composed a quick note before closing up the box and taping it. "C'mon, boys! We're going to go for a little walk to the post office!" she called.

"We did it!" Jennifer exulted, excitedly throwing her fists in the air after Casie had rounded up Landon and Jackson into the double stroller and then put shoes on her oldest son and walked out the door with him by her side as she pushed the stroller down the main street and toward the post office. "That's *got* to be a positive, right, Norbert? Dana and her daughter Molly are going to love that bear! That is definitely something of merit. I've never even heard of something so cool."

"Well, we'll have to wait and see," Norbert said. "I don't want you to get your hopes up, Darling. If making teddy bears were the ticket, people would be lining up at every sweatshop in China, begging for a job interview in the hopes of getting through the fabled pearly gates." But Norbert had a good feeling. He couldn't know that 700 miles away in a small town in Michigan, Dana Weston, courageous mother of the late baby Finley Weston and her rainbow baby Molly would receive a package in two days that would bring tears to her eyes and faith to her brimming heart. Neither Norbert nor Jennifer would see the look on Dana's face when she unwrapped the white tissue paper with little shamrocks on it to reveal a handcrafted teddy bear made of pastel dancing dinosaurs that smiled and tumbled all over its soft pajama body. They could not have felt the warm knot form in Dana's throat as she unfolded the neatly penned note and read:

Dear Dana and Molly,

Congratulations as you begin your journey as a family. Here is a keepsake from my home to yours. The story of your son has filled me with hope and faith that I will carry in my heart always—just as you will carry him always in yours. I think this little bear will feel very much at home with you and your daughter. Wishing you, your husband, and especially Molly, a lifetime of perfect smiles.

Cheering you on,

Casie, Landon, Jackson, and Finley.

At reading the last listed name, Dana dropped the paper in sheer disbelief, looking up at the sky in awe and amazement and shaking her head as if she couldn't believe what she was seeing.

Three of Jennifer Uccello's days took place when she was too young to make a difference. Sometimes, a cadet would arrive the same way—too young to carry out and perform the role of an initiate in the E.Z. Most Rev. 20s spent so much time on Earth, they couldn't wait to get their five days completed to experience what waited for them in the world beyond. Some, though, spent so little time on Earth, they had to wait for the right moment to say goodbye and let everyone there know that they were okay before they traveled onward. In these cases, fate would have to align so that the spirit of the very young had the chance to find the right medium to send its message. And such was the case that day for Finley Weston. His often-visited and flower-adorned headstone was engraved with only one date: August 4, 2014—the same day that Finley Gale was born to Casie 700 miles away in a sleepy, little town called Nazareth, Pennsylvania.

Jennifer was right. Today would be registered as a positive.

Chapter 11

"What's the matter with you, Patricia?" Norbert grumbled. "Are they sautéing some onions up in that little restaurant in the sky you've created for yourself?"

Patricia sniffed and wiped a tear that ran down her smooth, brown cheek. "Norbert—" she paused to collect herself. "I'll be honest with you, Sugar. I'm in a bit of shock here."

"Whatever are you talking about, Darling?" he continued derisively.

"I think you know what I'm talking about." She held out the Gale dossier to Norbert and then filed it away in a cabinet marked 'Positive.'

Norbert sighed and looked down and then quickly rummaged in his jacket pocket for a cigarette and lighter. "What's the big deal, anyway? Isn't that supposed to be what I'm doing up here? Making people's days?" He turned and walked silently away from Patty and down the long corridor toward his 'office.' Patty watched him as he left and then shook her head slowly.

"You know, they'll be waiting for you, Norbert!" she called out to him. But he was either too far away or too lost in thought to hear her.

•

"Jennifer?" Norbert called out to her in frustration. "Jennifer, how do I turn this damned thing on? I've been pressing this button over and over again, and nothing's happening."

Jennifer patiently walked over to where Norbert was sitting at his desk, fiddling with the new tablet that Patty had issued him a few weeks ago. "That's the camera lens. This," she explained, "is the back." She turned the tablet over in his hand so that it was facing the right way. "This is the front. There, see? Shiny side up. Now, push this little button on the bottom—"

"Oh, for God's sake!" Norbert grumbled. "Why would they make the back look so much like the front? Who the hell ever heard of such a thing? Give me my old paper dossiers and file cabinets back. Now, I'll be carrying this thing around like one of Jacob Marley's rusty ball and chains for the rest of eternity."

"It's pretty lightweight," Jennifer tried to be positive. She understood how difficult it was for Norbert to change his ways. "You'll get the hang of it eventually. Who do we have today?" she asked, trying to change the subject and take his focus away from his frustration with the new machine.

"I don't know. Stephen—something or other. I think I accidentally deleted the whole damn file when I was trying to make the screen bigger so I could see what the hell I was looking at. He's from Pennsylvania, but going to college over in Ohio somewhere—again with these Goddamned cold, northern states. He has a bunch a neutrals, maybe a negative—"

"Where in Ohio?" Jennifer asked, her ears perking up. "I'm from Ohio."

"Akron," Norbert answered, taking a deep drag from a newly lit cigarette and beginning to calm down. He waved the match quickly in the air to snuff out the flame. "Is that in your neck of the woods?"

"Not really. It's about an hour away." For the first time since she'd been in the E.Z., Jennifer's mind returned to her hometown. When her dad left, she and her mom had bounced around from place to place, and none of them ever really felt like home. When Jennifer got married, she and her ex-husband had a little starter home in Youngstown. They were practically kids, but they were able to buy a nice fixer-upper for almost nothing, using the money they'd gotten as wedding gifts for a down payment. Jennifer worked in a busy hair salon downtown, and her husband worked for an architecture firm in the city. Between her sense of style and his understanding of design and building, they had taken a pretty bland house and made it sparkle in the few short years that they were together. It sold within the first week of being on the market, which made the divorce proceedings finalize more quickly than either of them thought that they would. The last time she would see her ex-husband was at the closing. They both stayed relatively quiet and somber as they signed and initialed the dozens of papers in the lawyer's office, speaking only when prompted to, and authorizing the sale and transfer of their property. In each of their silent minds, they were remembering the excitement of the momentous day a few years ago when they first bought the little, old house. Their hearts were filled with hopeful uncertainty and promise as they excitedly counted the money out at the closing and received, in turn, the keys to what Jennifer hoped would be future bright enough to drown out a gray past.

Today, the sale of the house would cover about half of the legal fees for the divorce attorney. They would have to split the rest. "I'll be in touch," her ex had promised as he turned his back toward her and walked down the ramp of the building and over to where his blue Saab was parked neatly between the lines of the parking lot. Jennifer stoically regarded the car and watched it get smaller as it drove off, with a ribbon of wavy, blonde hair streaming condescendingly out of the slightly cracked passenger window, taking her hopes with it. She listened to the manual transmission shift smoothly and methodically from second to third, and from third to fourth as it disappeared down the street to the point where she could neither see it nor hear it anymore. And then she broke down and wept.

•

"...Jennifer...God almighty, I'm the one who's supposed to be losing my marbles here! Jennifer, is everything alright?"

Jennifer shook her head to clear her mind. She had lost herself in thought for a minute. "Sorry, Norbert," she said slowly. "I was just thinking about something."

"Well, let's start thinking about Stephen Whatever-the-hell-his-name-is so we can get today over with. Jeez, you had me going there, Jennifer! I was calling out your name for two minutes. You looked like you were in a trance! You need a cigarette or something, Darling?"

"I'm good, Norbert. Thanks." Jennifer smiled. Norbert always seemed to have a way of making her feel better. "Where do you keep getting those things anyway?" She laughed at his seemingly never-ending supply of cigarettes. "Is there a gas station around here that I don't know about?"

"Wouldn't that be nice? We could steal a car and get the hell out of here like Thelma and Louise in that movie."

Jennifer smiled.

"Actually, some thoughtful jerk must have put a pack in my casket with me at my viewing. They're not my brand, and the son-of-a-bitch game me menthols, but it's better than nothing. Somebody else must have given me these smoking cessation pills as a joke," he said, pulling a cylindrical orange tube out of the lined pocket on the interior of his jacket and shaking it like a rattle. "Probably my sister—she was always on my case about smoking. I used to tell her I'd quit when I was dead." He laughed to himself. "I've still got the whole damn bottle. I keep thinking maybe if I ever calm down enough around here, I might be able to quit one of these days. Course, I'd have had to bury my sister with a cask of wine the size of an oil drum to keep her busy in the afterlife if she were the one who went first. Thank God I did. I've got my old man's watch, too," he said, pulling on a chain from his pants pocket to reveal a polished and expensive-looking timepiece. "'Time waits for no one,' and all that crap he used to say. Can you believe those crazy Egyptians were right? We *can* take all this crap with us."

Jennifer had no pockets. She had no possessions. She came into the E.Z. with almost nothing. Of course, that's about what she left behind as well. The black dress, heels, and her grandmother's diamond earrings were the only tokens that remained from her life on Earth. *Life on Earth.* "Should we get going, Norbert?"

Norbert flippantly skidded the tablet across his desk as if he were playing shuffleboard with it. "Yeah, I'm ready to get the hell away from this place. I thought this was the Expiation Zone, not A Space Odyssey with all these kooky futuristic inventions. Let's go, Darling."

Chapter 12

"Lord, is this how college kids live these days?" Norbert asked as he surveyed the small apartment in front of him. "Casie Gale's toddlers were neat freaks compared to this guy." An open pizza box revealed a half-eaten crust that had been sitting on the coffee table for days. Beer bottles and cans spilled onto the floor from the counter tops and tables. Clothing was strewn all about the living room, and a television played video game music loudly for no one. Led Zeppelin and Pink Floyd posters covered the darkly paneled walls, and there was a stale and pungent odor of smoke in the air that even Norbert winced at. "What do you say we head to the library and borrow this kid some books on personal hygiene and recycling?" Norbert suggested, picking up a can from the kitchen table.

"We can't leave, Norbert. And we don't even know much about him. You left the tablet at the E.Z., remember? And you got so flustered that you deleted his file on accident anyway, so that won't help us. Can you remember anything? You said he had some neutrals, right?"

"Neutrals...maybe a negative...I'll be honest with you, Jennifer; I was so jazzed up about that Goddamned contraption Patricia gave me, I wasn't even thinking about the case file. I'm sorry."

"Ugh." Usually, Jennifer's demeanor was positive by default, and her first two successful cases as a Rev. 20 kept her sprits buoyed since she had been in the Expiation Zone. Still, there was something about her current surroundings that soured her mood this time around. Maybe it was being so close to home and all the aching memories that came along with it. She could almost feel the way that the roads would lead her reluctantly back if she followed them long enough. "Let's at least try to find this mysterious Stephen character and see what we can do for him."

She and Norbert waded through each room of the small, off-campus apartment. There were ashtrays, beer and alcohol bottles, mirrors and razor blades on virtually every flat surface in the place. Despite the unkempt surroundings, it was clear that the occupant was not short on cash. Flat 70" TVs hung in in the bedroom and living room. A Rolex watch was left next to a beer can filled with ashes on a bedside table. Wads of bills lay out in the open. Hundreds of dollars in gaming equipment, guitars, pedals, and amplifiers were strewn along the floor.

"I will, Ma! Get off my freakin' case, okay?" a voice suddenly came from the bathroom, followed by a crash as the phone smacked against the door and then plummeted dully to the ground. Norbert and Jennifer looked at one another.

"*I'm* not going in there," Jennifer mouthed to Norbert, shaking her head.

"Well, don't look at me," Norbert shook his head. Using the tips of two fingers, he lifted a shirt from one of the kitchen chairs and dropped it to the ground as if it were toxic waste. He then grudgingly sat down and took a cigarette out of his jacket pocket. "I wanted to go to the library."

Jennifer closed her eyes and breathed deeply. Adrien Cirillo was a police officer. Casie Gale was a mom. Both had spent their lives caring for the well-being of others. Patty had said that people who cultivated good energy were statistically going to be found doing something good with their lives when their five days came. Stephen was just a college student with a flair for music and video games and an apparent and serious addiction problem. She had no idea how she was going to make it out of this one with a 'positive,' and it didn't seem likely that Norbert was going to be of much assistance. Suddenly, a poisonous seed of doubt took root in her. Maybe it *was* just beginner's luck that allowed her to obtain two positives when she first arrived at the E.Z. What if Patty was wrong? What if, when the stakes were truly high and the task was really great, she was just mediocre after all? Lackluster. Neutral.

Her thoughts were broken by an abrupt thud from the bathroom. Jennifer and Norbert locked eyes again. Norbert shook his head, and Jennifer exhaled sharply. "I guess I'll have to do this by myself," she groused under her breath and clenched her jaw. She was furious with Norbert for not wanting to help, for leaving her to take care of everything.

"You know, you don't have to swing at every pitch, Darling," Norbert scoffed, feeling her frustration and exhaling the smoke from his cigarette.

Jennifer turned around sharply and faced him. "What's that supposed to mean, Norbert?"

"I mean, there are some people you just can't save. This kid's a bozo. He wants to die. I've seen this a hundred times. He's got that 'Poor Little Rich Kid' Syndrome. Look around this place, Jennifer. On a good day, this guy's a neutral—and even that's being generous." He gestured around the sordid apartment.

"Oh, so am I supposed to just give up like you, Norbert? Spend almost thirty years wasting my time away because I'm so full of my own self and my own fears that I can't bear the thought of helping somebody else make *his* future better? So worried about what's in it for me that I don't care about what it could mean for anyone else? Look at me, Norbert!" Jennifer gestured to herself. "I was 26 years-old when I died, not 72 like you. You spent your career dealing with death—burying your emotions along with people so you could wear fancy suits and drive around in Cadillacs and Lincolns your whole life; I hardly even got the *chance* to live mine!" All the frustration, the anger, the hurt, the guilt, the sadness of her brief 26 years washed over her like a wave, and she sank to her knees and sobbed. "Dammit, Norbert! What if my Rev. 20 was just phoning it in like you were when I needed him or her? This kid needs our help, and you're just sitting there with your arms folded like you're the only person in the Goddamned world!"

Norbert regarded her from across the room as her shoulders shook with tears that wracked her lean frame. He probably should have gone over to her and told her it would be alright. He probably should have said that he was sorry and assured her that even if this young man had all neutrals in his chart, he'd have another chance to atone in the Expiation Zone, just as she had when her time came. But, pride is the last thing to die in a person. It remains in the body long after the choroidal artery has been drained. How many times had Norbert buried it alive in people and sent it still pulsing into the afterlife? It still breathed in him even after all these years. "Oh, yes, Jennifer...my life was just as perfect as a cherry pie. I drove those hearses around like I was a kid playing on a giant, black carousel, listening to funeral dirges, smiling and happy as a clam. You have no idea what death will do to a person if you're around it long enough, Jennifer. You think being a funeral director is just raking in gobs of money while merrily burying little, old ladies who died peacefully in their sleep? You think there's no car accidents? No little kids sick with cancer? No horrible murders that would make your skin crawl? No grieving families so overcome with their own sadness that they can't bear to tear themselves away from the casket and they beg you to bury them, too? I'd have to ask people to *pinch* me so I didn't think I was dreaming and working in some amusement park for my whole life instead of a Goddamned funeral parlor, I was having so much ever-loving fun. You think trying to perk up *five* days is tough? Try 360 more of 'em—day after day, and year after year after year."

He stormed off and disappeared.

Jennifer couldn't see where he had gone. She collected herself and thought for a few minutes, preparing to shoot back another tirade at him, but her tongue was stopped by alarming sounds on the other side of the bathroom. She paused momentarily in dread and uncertainty, and then she grudgingly appeared on the other side of the door, where Stephen teetered forward and backward on his feet as he looked into the mirror with bloodshot eyes, trying desperately to focus on his reflection. White powder was lined up neatly in three rows on the bathroom vanity, and a bottle of pills sat with its cap open next to the sink. Beside him was a hastily scrawled note of goodbye.

"Stephen!" she screamed, voicelessly into the dank bathroom. Norbert's words filled her head, *"We can't touch them. We can't talk to them. But we can try to sway them to do something good so that their day gets registered as a positive. That's the name of the game, Darling."*

"Stephen!" she continued to scream, even though she knew he couldn't hear her. She tried to hold him back. He bent his face close to the vanity and toward the three thin, white lines meticulously placed on the surface. Her delicate arms whooshed helplessly through him like air. She fervently tried to block his mouth from gulping down the entire bottle of pills that he held in his hands, but he could only feel a cool breeze that seemed to flutter against his sweating forehead as his pulse raced and he collapsed onto the linoleum with a thud.

"Stephen! Stephen! Hello! Hello! Hello!"

Chapter 13

Jennifer's eyes flew open as if from a bad dream. Something inside her felt like a galloping racehorse. She put her hand to her chest, but felt nothing. She looked around and saw that she was back in the stark white of the Expiation Zone. In her mind, she ticked through the events of the past few hours, unsure if she had just had a nightmare or if she had truly witnessed what she had. There was so much about what she had just experienced that was unsettling to her: being back in Ohio, watching that young man take his life alone in the tiny, squalid bathroom apartment, fighting with Norbert.

Norbert. Of all the emotions that eddied and swirled around her, regret and guilt over the way that she talked to Norbert tugged at her with the most pull. She had never considered what it must have been like to be in his shoes. From what he had told her, his life was just as loveless and unhappy as hers was—and he'd lived more of it than she had. No wonder he kept to himself and refused to let anyone in. He made his living in a world governed by sadness, grief, and loss. She understood that he didn't want his eternal rest to be filled with the same thing. He had put up a wall to keep all the sadness out, and here he had just penned in himself, buried beneath his own fear of feeling. She felt like she had to apologize and try to make it right between them.

"Norbert!" she called out as she walked through the glass doors and into the office section of the E.Z., passing each cubicle along the way. "Norbert, I'm sorry," she said as she finally reached the end, and gently put her hand on the blue blazer covered shoulder of the man who sat with his back to her in the last cubicle in the row.

At the touch of her hand, the man turned around. He was middle aged, with wild blond hair and a cheap tie. A nametag that read "Don's House of Cars" was pinned above his left chest pocket. "Hello, there! Name's Don Kane from Don's House of Cars. I'm new here!" He held out a large paw-like hand out for Jennifer to shake. She shook her head slowly in disbelief and began backing away from him.

"Where's Norbert?" she asked softly.

"I'm not sure," Don replied. "There's a nice lady named Patty that told me this would be my office. Some place, huh?"

Patty! Angry tears streamed down Jennifer's face as she ran back past the cubicles, out the glass office door, past Norbert's smoking 'office,' and into the lobby of the Expiation Zone. She was panting by the time she got to Patty, her toes nearly slipping out from the black stiletto heels. "Patty!" she called, trying to catch her breath. "What's going on?"

Patty turned around from her files to see Jennifer looking ragged and war torn. Tears streamed down her face, creating lines of gray along her porcelain cheeks. "Baby, baby…," she said, holding her arms out toward Jennifer. "What's the matter, Sugar?"

"I hate this place!" Jennifer exclaimed. "You're supposed to be the Resident Guide. Guide me! Tell me what's going on here! I tried so hard! I tried so hard to do everything for those people: Adrien, Casie. I wanted them to have the chance that I didn't. But now—Stephen—it's just not fair!"

"What are you talking about, Jennifer?"

Jennifer was still too caught up in emotion to be reasoned with. Her words kept coming out of her mouth in a torrent. "Maybe Norbert was right. This place is nothing but a Godforsaken hellhole. And where is God in all of this anyway, huh? Where's God! Ever since I've been here, it seems like everyone else is doing all the work to try to get these poor people where they need to go. There's no God anywhere to be found. And I failed! I failed."

"Whoa, whoa, whoa, Sugar! You need to take a deep breath and slow down. Don't you go offending God now, Baby. And what are you talking about? You're doing a great job up here."

Jennifer sniffled and took a breath. "Well, where is God? Where was God when Stephen killed himself in his bathroom and there was nothing I could do to stop him? Where was God when I died somehow at only 26 years-old and woke up here?"

"Oh, Baby. I don't have all the answers, but you've got to open your eyes a little bit." Patty gestured with her hands. "This has more to do with God than you realize. Who do you think picks out your case files and puts them in the dossiers? Who do you think picks out the five days?"

Jennifer paused in her crying. She hadn't considered this.

"Everything that happens here is God, Baby," Patty assured her. Jennifer sniffled again.

"But, what about Stephen? And why the hell is there some used car salesman in Norbert's cubicle?"

"What do you mean, Sugar?" Patty asked, confused. "You must have known that yesterday's positive was Norbert's fifth day. Didn't he tell you?"

Jennifer shook her head. "I don't know what you're talking about, Patty. We failed. Norbert and I failed that mission. Stephen killed himself. There's no way that was a positive. And Norbert disappeared, and I...I couldn't stop Stephen from...I couldn't stop him..." Her voice trailed off as she mentally recounted the scene from her point of view with shame and horror.

She didn't see what happened on the other side of the closed door in the moments before she arrived in the bathroom. She didn't see the part where Norbert took a giant breath, knowing that, if everything worked out, this would be his fifth day. She didn't see him hastily smear away the cocaine and replace it with perfectly lined baby powder that stretched along the vanity. She didn't see him take the bottle of Oxycodone, throw it out the window, pull something from his jacket pocket, and leave a similar-looking orange cylinder full of woefully expired and relatively harmless smoking cessation pills in its place. Didn't see him clumsily curse the buttons on the phone that looked to him like a miniature version of Patricia's tablet, as he redialed Stephen's mother and pressed the button on the screen that looked like a loudspeaker. Jennifer didn't hear over her own screaming of Stephen's name, his mother calling out through the speaker of the phone, "*Stephen! Stephen! Hello! Hello! Hello!*" And hear him lethargically regain consciousness as his mother said she was calling for help. And hear him vow to come home. And go back to counseling. And never go back to the drugs again.

And mean it.

PART II-NOX

Chapter 14

Ah, come on, Buddy! You've got a family! Jennifer scrolled, frustrated, with her finger along the document in the tablet and poured over the information in front of her regarding the case who appeared on her dossier this morning. It had been two days since the events in Akron, Ohio.

"You're going to do just fine, Baby," Patty had promised her. "I told you that you were a natural, and I wasn't just whistling Dixie when I said it either. You're as sweet as a beignet, sharp as a tack, and you've got a good heart. You just follow that heart, Sugar. It'll lead you to where you're going. And don't you worry about ol' Mr. Norbert. I don't know anyone who understands death better than that old coot did. Lord knows where he went off to, but he's going to be just fine, too."

Jennifer wasn't sure. She had spent the last two days mentally reviewing everything that she could remember from the hazy moments when she first appeared in the Expiation Zone. She tried desperately to recount as much as she could of her life up until her final day, but it was all hazy and out of sequence—like trying to recall a memory from early childhood. The best she could do was cobble together bits and pieces, but she wasn't sure if she was just making them up or if they ever really occurred. The end of her life had become just as foggy as the very beginning. She remembered a lot of sadness in the days following the sale of the house in Youngstown. She remembered working long hours, picking up extra shifts where she could to try to keep busy and to make a little bit of extra cash. She remembered moving boxes from her house into a friend's apartment temporarily until she could find a place that she could afford on her own. How much time went by in that span? A month? A few weeks? A few days? As much as she strained to remember, it was gone.

She chose instead to focus on her role in the Expiation Zone. Having completed three successful missions, she was no longer an initiate, but an official Revelation 20. There was a part of her that was proud of this, and still a small part that regarded it with the same sense of disinterest and indifference that Norbert might have. Maybe Norbert wasn't exactly the best cheerleader when it came to encouraging her to shift the outcome of the days on her caseload, but she technically had never completed a mission without him, and she was scared. In Riverwoods and Nazareth, she and Norbert had worked together as a team, but Akron—well, that was *all* Norbert. She smiled a bit wistfully as she reviewed the coordinates for her upcoming placement. Norbert would have loved this newest mission. Alabama in spring. Nice and warm. She thought of Norbert and that crazy story that he had told her about the little bird sharpening its beak and wearing down that giant mountain.

"Got yourself a good placement, huh?"

A confident, masculine voice broke through her thoughts. She turned around and looked up to see the face of a man of about 30 years of age peering down at her from behind. Wavy, black hair framed his chiseled cheekbones, and a dimple formed at each side of his mouth as he grinned, revealing perfectly white teeth. His dark eyes were hidden under the thick black of his eyebrows and the mop of glistening hair.

"Uh…" Jennifer was speechless. She wasn't sure who this person was or where he had come from. "What placement?"

"You know…the Bridge?" He self-assuredly took the tablet from her hand and began scrolling though it to review her casefile.

"Hey!" she yelled, grabbing the tablet back from him, feeling a jolt shoot through her as her hand briefly touched his. "What are you doing? Don't touch that. It's mine."

"Okay, fine." He plopped himself on the edge of her desk. "I just saw you smiling from over in my cubicle, and I wanted to see what it was that was finally making you happy. You usually look so serious and sad. I thought maybe they were sending you off to the Maldives to cheer you up or something."

Jennifer regarded him warily. She had never seen him before, but she had been so focused on her work and her own confusion that she admittedly hadn't paid much attention to her surroundings in the office section of the E.Z. He was wearing a crisp white button-down shirt and black dress pants. A rolled-up tie snaked out of the pocket of his dress shirt, and a gold watch was perched boldly on his strong wrist. He looked as if he could have just stepped out of a photo shoot for a magazine or movie premier. Smiling was his default, and the dimples that framed his mouth seemed a constant on his face, but there was an air of mischief in the dark slant of his eyes.

"Well, they're not sending me there. And even if they were, it would be none of your business," Jennifer shot back.

The young man was unphased. "Feisty, huh? I like it."

Jennifer rolled her eyes. She was often relieved that she had married young when guys like this one would come into the salon. The wedding band was usually enough to fend off their flirts and advances, but she still sometimes had to endure the taunts that came from a few skirt-chasing guys who just didn't seem to know when to take the hint.

"Come on…live a little…oh, wait…" he patted his chest and made a mock attempt at checking for a pulse on his wrist. For the first time, a wry grin formed on Jennifer's stony face. It was *kind of* funny.

"There it is. I see it. I see it. She can smile."

In spite of herself, Jennifer smiled at him. "Very funny," she said, dryly. Something that he had said caught her interest. "Why do you call it 'the Bridge'?"

"Well, that's what it is, isn't it? We can't get to the other side without crossing it, right?"

Jennifer hadn't thought of that.

"I'm Nox Reyes." He held out his hand. Jennifer reluctantly reached for it and again felt a surge as she felt the firmness of his grip. "Pleasure to meet you." He smiled again, and Jennifer studied him with guarded eyes in silence. "Jeez! Did that old cat, Norbert, steal your tongue or something? You can talk to me, you know," Nox continued.

At this, Jennifer bristled. "What about Norbert?" she asked haughtily.

"Hey, easy…no offense," Nox said, backing off slowly. "I just saw you hanging around with him last week, that's all. Crazy lunatic. Where is he, anyway? Out for a smoke break?"

Jennifer remained quiet and began to build the wall around herself, stone by stone. For some inexplainable reason, she felt a certain need to protect Norbert. He had never done any harm to her, and she didn't like to hear anyone say anything disparaging about him, let alone this cocky stranger.

Nox seemed to sense that he had pushed the boundary too far. "Hey, look. I'm sorry if I offended you, okay? It's just…I worked with Norbert. Or, I guess you could call it 'working.' He wasn't exactly head of the labor union around here; you know what I mean?"

Jennifer suddenly remembered bits of the conversation she'd overheard between Patty and Norbert when she first arrived in the E.Z. *"That last one you sent me could have modeled for GQ, and look at the way that whole mess turned out—" Was Norbert talking about Nox?* She decided to pretend that she had no idea what Nox was talking about and to listen to his side of the story.

"That old coot was clueless. And who smokes anymore? I felt like I was on fire every time I got near him. I could barely breathe around him, let alone work. I can't stand the smell of cigarettes—I'm allergic to them. Well, I've been doing just fine without him. I nailed two out of the last five missions since he and I split."

Jennifer filed away this piece of information and chose not to brag that her record was 3-0. Nox seemed only too happy to fill the air with his own voice anyway, and she was glad that she didn't have to share much more information about herself or her relationship with Norbert. She and Norbert hadn't exactly left on good terms, and she still felt a pang of guilt when she thought about how he had sacrificed his time in the Expiation Zone to save Stephen, and how she never got to say that she was sorry.

"I have a knack for numbers with this whole 'five days' thing, and I love being back on the old globe anyway. I get a rush out of each new place. I've spent the last few months traveling abroad before I got here, so this is like old hat for me, you know. Course this place isn't exactly getting the best reviews on Trip Advisor as far as accommodations go, but what are you going to do, right? The décor could use some updating." He motioned to the stark white walls. Everything in the Expiation Zone was bland and colorless and came off as more sterile than serene. "I was in marketing as the Vice President of Acquisition for Solugrid—it's this giant energy firm. We're an American Company, but they relocated me to the European market to work on some future accounts over there. We put up a lot of plants, some windmills, stuff like that—mostly petroleum pipelines. A lot of people don't like seeing power plants and pipelines coming to their villages, so my boss would send a young, charming guy like me in to help the locals see the benefits and encourage town councils to buy in. Professional relations, you know."

Oh, Jennifer knew. She'd seen and heard about projects that kept popping up along the "rust belt" in the United States. Always the same story: jobs for locals, booming benefits. It all seemed pretty short-sighted to her when she considered the numerous risks that came along as the plants began dotting towns all around the country. Seems like it was the same story everywhere.

"The energy gig is just a big numbers game anyway—risk analysis, predicting likelihood, downplaying consequences, making things work in our favor. So, this 'five days' stuff is my forte," Nox continued. "Taking what you have lying around and making it work so that the people see the world the way you want them to see it. It's really no different from what I was doing at Solugrid—except I can't talk to or touch anybody. Good thing those rules don't apply up here in the Expiation Zone, huh?" he said, winking at her.

Jennifer bristled and rolled her eyes. "What a shame you left the world so soon," she said dryly. "It sounds like they really needed you down there conning unsuspecting villagers into building more energy-efficient pipelines though their backyards so that you and your company could make billions. I'd love to know what caused your unfortunate demise."

"It's no mystery," Nox declared, surprisingly. "What's the big secret? It's all technology nowadays, baby. We leave a digital trail like a slug. You've got the keys to the kingdom right there in your hand," he said, nodding his head at her chest, where she was still clutching her tablet closely. "I know how to figure it out."

"How is that…possible…?" Jennifer took the bait. She wanted to know how Nox had used his tablet to figure out how he had died, but before she had finished her sentence, he had completely vanished.

Chapter 15

In an old city in the Sheki region of Azerbaijan, along the Caucasus Mountains, presidents, prime ministers, and some CEOs from several small countries in Eastern Europe quietly met at a hotel that overlooked the natural sulphur hot springs of the idyllic village below. Amid the tantalizing aroma of spicy, lemony lamb kebabs and the cool glasses of black tea sherbet, a young man surveyed the view from the balcony of the ballroom. The snow-capped, rugged mountains interrupted the clouds, and far below, a river snaked through verdant hills. Small dots of huts broke the landscape to one side of the panoramic view, and pointed cathedrals constructed thousands of years ago still stood on the rolling hilltop on the other side of the vista. He could see for many, many miles from the windy perch on the balcony.

Unseen was the constant armed conflict between two ethnic groups that created more of a border than the rivers and mountains did in this ancient town. This quiet, restful location had fallen out of favor with most tourists, who preferred the glitz of Baku to the quiet solitude of the majestic mountains near the old city. The topic of discussion between the dignitaries on this particular evening was the construction of a petroleum pipeline that would span the Anatolian region from Turkey, through Georgia and Azerbaijan, beneath the Caspian Sea, and into Turkmenistan, ideally bringing large profits to every country that it traversed. A dozen energy companies had sent ambassadors to woo the dignitaries in the hopes of getting a piece of the eastern European energy pie. The American Vice President from an enterprising energy company called Solugrid milled about the room, eyeing the Prime Minister of Georgia. His was the last signature that was needed to begin the bidding process of restructuring the pipelines that would cut through the region. Landing this contract would mean billions for Solugrid—and a cozy commission for the young man.

"*Eezveeneete. Ya plokha favaryoo pa rooskee. Vig gavareetye pa angleeskee?*" the young man stammered slowly to one of the caterers who was milling around holding a tray of appetizers in his hand.

"Probably better than you do," the attendant replied snidely in a heavy European accent. "You Americans and your Rosetta Stone...What is it that you want?"

"Hahaha. Sorry," the American replied somewhat sheepishly. "It's my first time in this country. That gentleman there," he continued, pointing slightly at the suave figure in the black suit. "I'd like to buy him a drink if that's possible."

•

"Patty?" Jennifer called out, walking toward the desk in the lobby of the Expiation Zone.

"Right here, Sugar!" Patty answered, her large rear end rising up from where she was hidden behind the desk, putting a folder into the lowest drawer of a filing cabinet marked 'negatives.' "How can I help you?"

Jennifer averted her gaze from Patty's behind and focused on the red lettering of the file cabinet. She hadn't noticed it before. "Are there many 'negatives' that come through here?" she asked, briefly changing the topic of her initial question.

"Sugar, I see all kinds of things come through here. These new tablets are supposed to make this process easier, but I still find myself on the floor from time to time alphabetizing everything until we're at 100% with this new technology. I think I'm seeing double half the time. I swear, sometimes I think ol' Miss Culpepper had the right idea doing everything the old-fashioned way with her stationary set and that fancy gold pen of hers. Reading through these digital copies only to have to print them out and file 'em away anyway is running me ragged! I feel like I'm doing twice the work as I—"

"I'm sorry, Patty. I didn't mean to interrupt."

"No. No, Sugar. I really have all the time in the world. How can I help you today? I see you're heading down to Alabama for your fourth mission.

That's a nice place for you! If I was you, I would get yourself some nice Lowcountry Boil while you're down there! Mmmmm…I had a sister that moved out there when she got married the second time, and she was always ravin' about the soul food they had in Alabama and how I had to get myself over there for a visit because the biscuits were the size of a cat's head. But I tol' her I was just as happy to be in New Orleans with my crawfish boil and jambalaya and that I'd rather stay home and eat an alligator raw than to go hoppin' across the Mississippi just for some doughy biscuits bigger than God intended them to be—and I wasn't exactly in a hurry to see that lowdown husband of hers—"

"Patty," Jennifer interrupted softly. "What do you know about Nox Reyes?"

"Nox Reyes? Mmmmmmm…he's that good-lookin' boy that ran out on ol' Norbert a few weeks ago. He's got himself a record, Miss Jennifer. And I thought Norbert was bad! Dear Lord, if that boy's not careful, he's gonna get kicked out of here and sent to where it's nice and warm year-round, if you know what I mean."

Jennifer was confused. Nox had been bragging about how he'd had two successful missions already. Of course, she didn't know him well enough to know if he was being honest when he said this or not. Actually, it would figure that he would be lying to try to impress her and she was too naïve to notice. Afterall, he made his living downplaying the numbers and inflating the benefits of non-renewable energies. This was a drawback of marrying so young—Jennifer still thought that everyone maintained the innocence that she did, and she was often disappointed to find that they didn't.

"Right here," Patty testified, taking a folder back out of the 'negative' filing cabinet. "This is confidential information, but I just had to put two 'negatives' away for that chil' last week alone. Lord, I know Norbert was supposed to be training him, and ol' Mr. Norbert might not have had the best track record, but I've never seen more slip-ups like this back-to-back before. I think ol' Mr. Norbert got so many neutrals because I swear he just didn't like to be bothered, and he was afraid of changing his crazy ways. His files used to come back after 24 hours with his activity record showing nothing but a few dozen smoke breaks. But Nox! Well, it's almost like this good-lookin' fellow is trying to goof things up. He's been zooming way off course of the mission just about every time. Although, I can't imagine who in the world would want to do that! Lord, I been dotting every 'i' and crossing every 't' just in the hopes that when my two years is up and I done served my penance as Resident Guide, I'm going to be reunited with my Mama, and we're gonna spend some good quality time sitting on a porch in some rockin' chairs, just going over what she's seen and where she's gone, and I'll tell her about my son, and find out whatever happened to Daddy and Uncle Linus..."

Jennifer backed away from Patty, who was no longer paying her any attention, but was instead absentmindedly sorting through folders and talking about what she was going to do when she saw her mother again in the Empire. Jennifer turned and walked with a determined gait back through the glass doors of the office section of the E.Z. and toward her cubicle. In the starkness and weightlessness of the E.Z., a feeling began to take over the lightness of her body. And it burned like fire.

Chapter 16

"The key word is 'risk.' Do you follow me?" the American continued in his animated tone. His dark eyes twinkled, and he smiled with one side of his mouth, causing a dimple to break the perfection of his chiseled cheek. "It's a numbers game. There's an economic benefit for you, and there's a marginal risk possibility for the—albeit small—community that lies *just* outside the region if nothing is done to the existing structure. Sure, you might save a few million by simply bolstering or re-armoring the currently existing pipeline, but just think of the safety measures that you can enact if you construct a brand new—and significantly larger—one instead. Surely, the calculation of risk is important to you in the bidding process. My company has found a way to assess the consequences so that proposed risk is smaller—and your profits are higher than they would be with our nearest competitor." The American smiled again.

The Prime Minister regarded him darkly. He had a distaste for the American—and his American company—but the savings *were* significant, as was the promised 'perk' that he would personally take home if he agreed to sign for the bid. "And what about the risk of failure?" he asked in his slow, husky voice. "There are people who have been on this land for generations. Big companies have been pulling oil out of these mountains since the 1800s, and the people of Georgia are already feeling distrustful of our government and what we are doing with the oil. They are convinced there will be trouble if we try to change the structure from what currently stands there."

"Think of the odds of getting struck by a car on a new highway as opposed to an old one," The American continued. "There is a small chance that someone might be hit and killed by a driver on a motorway, right? But no more so than it would be on an old highway. Would that prevent a country from building a new road that will also provide easy transportation to millions of people and significant commerce to your city? Think of the gains to your country's industry! Think of the positions that you can offer to the people of Georgia—especially those who are struggling financially. Think of how increasing transit would enable them to have a better life, and how it would be foolish to refuse to even pursue the option because there is a trivial risk to a very marginal population of less than .078% that *might* potentially be struck by a motorcar—hypothetically speaking, of course. The benefits outweigh the cost—the perceived cost—and the benefits are concrete, sir. That, I can guarantee you. And let's not forget the *personal* benefit that my company is willing to offer to *you* in particular—if you simply agree to allow us to start the bidding process with your nation." The young man winked, smiled, and stuck out his hand. The Prime Minister regarded it carefully, his eyes narrowing.

●

"There you *are*!" Nox crowed as Jennifer walked toward her cubicle. "I was looking all over for you."

Jennifer jumped at the sound of his voice. "Well, you found me, so can stop looking. And you can stop talking to me, too. What's your story anyway?" she demanded. "What are you trying to do here? I was talking to Patty just a minute ago, and she said you had two 'negative' days already and keep veering off course. Just what kind of trick are you trying to pull?"

"Whoa…slow down, sister. You doing a little outside research or what? If you have questions, you can ask *me* instead of going over to Patty." He smiled at her as she began walking away from him. "I'm an open book."

"Well, then I am asking you," Jennifer demanded, turning toward him angrily. "Why did you get two negatives last week?"

"Hey, take it easy, okay? Let's not be too hasty to judge, little Miss Revelation 20, lest the measure you use against me be used against you, too. Not everyone hits a grand slam on their first at bat. Maybe I'm just not lucky like you are. How many points have *you* racked up?"

Jennifer backed off a bit. In her life, she had been anything but lucky, and the five neutral days she earned were hardly anything that she could control if she had wanted to. Maybe it was possible that Nox's 'negatives' were truly just a result of the bad luck of being assigned to people who simply were impossible to save. Nox studied her face and smiled. Some ancient, instinctive reaction in Jennifer forced her face to smile back. Besides, Nox had something that she wanted. "I'm sorry," she said softly. "I think we may have gotten off on the wrong foot. I'm Jennifer Ucc—"

"I know who you are," Nox smiled again and raked his hand over his black, wavy hair to reveal his twinkling dark eyes. "You stand out here." Jennifer looked around as if for the first time and noticed the other Revelation 20s. She and Nox were significantly younger than most of the other people who filled the cubicles of the E.Z. "But, then again, you'd probably stand out anywhere," he added as if he could read her thoughts.

Jennifer's eyes met his, and again she was filled with fire. She looked away quickly and focused instead on her tablet, hoping he hadn't picked up on how uncomfortable she felt when their eyes met. "I have to get to work," she said, looking at the time at the top of her screen. Six of the twenty-four hours that she had to complete this mission had already lapsed, and she wasn't sure that she should waste any more time on Nox—even if he did seem to have a knack for technology and might be able to help her.

"A star-player like you?" Nox continued. "You could swoop in at quarter to midnight and probably still save the day. Why don't you relax a little bit? We can stroll through the grounds of the Expiation Zone, talk about the Empire, swap battle stories. Hey…I can even show you that little hack I know to get a glimpse of your last day if you want."

Once again, it was as if he could read her thoughts. Jennifer tried to act demure and calm as she clutched her tablet closely and looked down at the back of it where the small logo of the iconic silver apple with one bite taken from it shone. What was it about forbidden knowledge that is always so hard to resist?

Chapter 17

"First off, do a little personal reflection," Nox explained, eyeing Jennifer's form-fitting black dress and heels. They were walking together along the long corridor of the Expiation Zone, where Norbert had his secret smoking office. "I bet you died from a tragic jump-rope incident gone wrong. You really should have known better than to wear those shoes while working out. Do you always go to the gym dressed like that?" he joked with a smirk.

"I might," Jennifer answered. "How about you? Were you cycling through Europe in that tuxedo when you pompously ignored a sign saying that a bridge was out and plummeted tragically off a cliff?" For the first time, it occurred to Jennifer that the two of them created a rather attractive and unorthodox couple under the circumstances. Amid the work clothes, dowdy hospital gowns, or pajamas that many of the Revelation 20s were wearing, Nox and Jennifer looked like they were going to some afterlife version of the prom together. She still could not imagine why she was so dressed up when she died.

"The last thing *I* remember was being in Russia. I flew into Moscow and did some sightseeing before heading down to Azerbaijan. My boarding pass, my bus tickets, the reservation for the walking guided tour of the

Caucasus Mountains—it's all here in my email. I was able to hack into it through a loophole in the settings of the tablet. The activity stops on March 22, so I know that must have been my last day. It's simple," Nox remarked, scrolling down the screen and highlighting buttons on his own tablet.

"But *how* did you die?" Jennifer pressed. "How? How does a young person like you just die? What are you, like, 30 years old?"

"Good guess. Thirty-one—"

"So, how does someone who appears to be in the prime of his life just cease to exist at thirty-one years of age?"

Nox looked at her squarely. "I still exist." His tone was uncharacteristically cold. He reached out and ran his finger along her jaw slowly, and Jennifer felt every hair on her stand as if pulled by a magnet. "See?" He moved in close to Jennifer's face and dropped his voice to a low, husky whisper. "Do you think knowing how you died is going to change the fact that you did?" Jennifer held her breath, and he continued, "Is it going to get you across the bridge any faster? Is it going to help you sleep any better at night in a place like this where nights and days are just twenty-four hours spent for someone else that you're trying to live through when you can't live for yourself anymore?" He pulled back. "You're dead, baby. And now you get five days. That's how you exist."

Jennifer backed up and drew in a deep, deep breath. Her lungs filled with icy air, and she exhaled slowly. Breathing here was different. There were moments on Earth where she'd held her breath going through tunnels, or while rising up a steep rollercoaster, or while stealing quick gasps during the rest in a song. Sometimes, she would just watch in the silence of a sleepless night as her chest rose and fell with each effortless inhalation and exhalation as her body worked naturally, effortlessly, instinctively to keep itself alive even on those dark, sad nights after the divorce when she'd wished that it wasn't. Now, it went on through the same rhythmic impulse as the freezing air moved in and out of her lifeless body to keep her dead. Nox's words played on repeat in her mind. *"Do you think knowing how you died is going to change the fact that you did?"* And somewhere in the deep, primordial part of her where the breath, and the cells, and the energy still pulsed in spite of her soul's new surroundings, a silent syllable sounded.

Yes.

•

"So, it's a 'yes,' then?" Nox prattled, triumphantly. His firm hand gripped determinedly around the other hand in an affirmation of agreement. "Let's get started on this right away. I've been working out the kinks of this for weeks, so I know all of the ins and outs of this process. There's nothing that you'll need to worry about. I'll just require a little bit of information from you to get started, and then we'll get to work on this as early as—well, let's start right now. Trust me, you will not be sorry that you've agreed to this. It's a win-win for both of us."

Still, each knew that nothing could be further from the truth.

Chapter 18

"Nurse, where is my stationary set? I'd like to write a letter to my brother, Leroy."

"Oh, you sit down now, Miss Culpepper," the plump home-health nurse entreated, easing the frail, white-haired woman back into her armchair. Thin golden bangles clanked together against the bruised, crepey purple and white skin that covered the fragile radius and ulna of the elderly woman like a cheetah's coat. She kept her hair styled and wore her good jewelry in an attempt to conceal her mounting age, but her giant diamond solitaire ring just swiveled loosely around the bulbous knuckles that punctuated her skeletal, long, pink-tipped fingers, and the perfectly groomed silver white waves of her hair were barely enough to cover the forehead below.

The large, blue-clad nurse patted Miss. Culpepper lightly on her lean shoulder, where the blade stuck out almost like a dorsal fin. "I'll get that stationary out for you in just a minute. It's lunch time right now. I made you some nice red beans and rice to help you put some meat on those bones of yours, Missy. You know, I had to do something with all the pork that was left over from yesterday—you hardly touched your dinner last night. You're not feeling poorly are you, Miss Culpepper? You usually love when I make you a nice pork dinner on a Wednesday night. I was surprised to find you ain't touched a morsel of it this morning when I came in to check your medicine in the refrigerator. Well, don't you worry—I didn't add too much spice to it, and I left out the ham because I know you think it makes it too salty, and—"

"Is it Wednesday?" the frail voice interrupted quietly.

"No, ma'am, it's Thursday. Thursday at noon, and it's time for you to sit down and let me get you a nice plate of that red beans and rice I was telling you about. I soaked the beans all last night, and I cut the amount of peppers in it from four to one the way my mama called for it in her recipe—'cause I know you don't like it too spicy. Now, my mama used to put a little splash of cider vinegar in each bowl before dishing out the beans. She always said cider vinegar would help a body live to be a hundred and three, and she was darn close to makin' it, too, let me tell you—"

"Because you usually wear purple on Thursdays," the aged southern voice interrupted again. "You're in blue, so I thought it was Wednesday today."

The plump nurse looked down. Indeed, she was in her blue scrubs. "Lord above, you don't miss a trick, do you, Miss Culpepper? I must have laid out my clothes all wrong this morning! I been so distracted talking on the phone in the mornings with my sister griping about that husband of hers. I keep telling her that if he really loved her, he would get off of that useless rump of his and find some honest work to do, and that she could be poor by herself if she really wanted to struggle so badly, and she doesn't need his two-timing help to do it! But she don't want to hear none of it. 'I love him' and this and that. Well, I tol' her that I got room in my house if she ever wants to come back and live home with me, but she keeps saying she can't leave him, and—"

"And your medicine," the frail voice trembled. "Don't you usually take your medicine when you bring me my tea in the morning? I didn't hear you shaking that bottle like you usually do."

Patty stopped and pressed her lips together. She moved her right hand up and patted the uncharacteristically empty spot by her chest. She tried to think of where her medicine bottle was. She must have left it in the little pocket on the left side of the top of the blue set of scrubs that she wore yesterday. The one closest to her heart, where today the lipid bilayer of the cells surrounding the organ detected a change in the viscosity that routinely affected the rotation of its working. Because she had skipped two doses of medicine, the statins that usually kept the membranes stabile and controlled had not reported for duty this morning, and the environment in her chest cavity was steadily, though imperceptibly changing and thickening with the southern heat and the usual stress of the day. Deep inside, at the cellular level, each beat of Patricia's heart would bring it closer to a final countdown that would end abruptly just before she cleared the picked-at dishes of Miss. Culpepper's barely-eaten dinner later that evening.

"And the gold pen," Miss. Culpepper continued in her stammering southern drawl. "I'd like to write a letter to my brother, Leroy."

"Now, now, Miss Culpepper," Patricia said, forgetting about her own medicine and focusing back on her elderly charge. "You just set down and take a nice bite of my red beans and rice." For all its internal compromises and unknown struggles, Patricia's heart couldn't find it in itself to break the daily reminder to Mrs. Culpepper that her brother Leroy had died more than fifty years ago.

•

"Hi, Patty…"

Patricia spun around quickly at her desk in the Expiation Zone, clutching at her chest in surprise. "Oh, well hello there, Mr. Nox. How are you this afternoon? Lord God Almighty, but if you didn't just scare me half to death for a second time. Hoo! You know, it's funny you found me here because I've been wondering about you and your missions. Is everything going alright with you? I know your mentor Mr. Norbert is no longer available, but after two unsatisfactory missions, it is part of protocol to set you up with another seasoned Revelation 20 who might be able to help you."

"I was hoping you'd say that," Nox cooed, flashing her a mischievous smile that made his dimples dig into each side of his rugged cheeks. "I think it might be a good idea if I try the whole 'mentorship' thing again. You know…maybe join in on a mission with someone as an apprentice so I can learn the trade a little more thoroughly?" Patty nodded her head slowly in agreement. A wavy black wisp of hair spilled down over Nox's forehead and covered his eyes, and he continued, "I was thinking maybe Jennifer could help me."

Patricia's bright lips turned down, and her warm chocolate eyes narrowed. "Miss Jennifer?" she asked in surprise. "Nox, Miss Jennifer hasn't even been here as long as you have. She's not a veteran Revelation 20 by any means—"

"Yeah…" Nox dismissed, nonchalantly. "But she said I could come with her on her next mission if it was okay."

"Miss Jennifer said that?" Patricia looked out of the corner of her eye to where Jennifer sat, oblivious to Nox's scheme, at the coffee table across from the reception area and the lobby desk, reviewing her tablet, trying to find any trace of old emails that she might have sent or received, and making final plans for her mission to Alabama. Sensing that someone was looking at her, Jennifer looked up and saw that it was Patty. She smiled and waved unwittingly at her before returning her gaze back to the tablet.

"See?" Nox said in a low whisper so that Jennifer couldn't hear. "She said it was no problem as long as it was alright with you."

"Well, I don't see why not," Patty continued uncertainly. "Let me just make a few adjustments in the system."

"I'll take care of it," Nox offered, waving his hand in dismissal. "I don't want to take you away from what you're doing. Really. It's no big deal— I'll just tag along with her on her next mission. I've got it all under control. That was a good idea, Patty, letting Jennifer help me get some extra pointers and a few more missions under my belt. You're such a good Resident Guide, you know that? Thank you."

"You're…welcome…," Patricia faltered, slowly, trying to remember when she had said that pairing Nox up on a mission with Miss Jennifer was her idea, but Nox was walking away from her before she had the chance to question him or think about it for too much longer.

Despite touting that it would bring numerous jobs in each of the cities in which its plants were built, the interview process at Solugrid was a rigorous one for outside applicants, and positions were frequently filled by those who already had ties to the company or to those with ties to people with connections to land interests that Solugrid was looking to obtain. Candidates for production, manufacturing, and engineering would need to be in possession of at least a master's degree in engineering or its related fields. They must submit three letters of recommendation in addition to the usual transcripts from prestigious institutions, and there was an ideal work experience minimum of five to ten years in the environmental sector. Following two initial baseline interviews, applicants without ties or without preexisting connections to the company were subject to a third interview with the president of Solugrid. This final hurdle served as a personality screening. Before reviewing any vitaes or resumes, the president asked the same question of the engineers as was asked of the custodians, secretaries, or marketing staff: "Can you describe for me a situation in which you would make an important decision without having all of the required information to do it?"

At this question, Nox Reyes reached across the president's desk and took his cover letter and resume from her hands. Her heart skipped as he crumpled the premium ivory paper in his strong hands, eyed her mischievously, and smiled so that his dimples etched at each side of his mouth. "Sure. I'll describe a situation like that: You hire me," he directed confidently, as he threw the balled-up resume into the mesh canister next to her desk, "and then we can decide what we're going to do with all of the success that Solugrid experiences once we join forces and take on the world together."

Chapter 19

"Jeez Louise! You waiting on an important call or something? You know, the phone stops ringing for you once you've crossed over, darling. And not that I care, but what the hell is Solugrid? You've been muttering about it since you got here." Norbert took a drag on his cigarette and exhaled its gray smoke in the face of the handsome, dark-haired initiate who was sitting on the subway car next to him, staring intently at his phone.

The young man picked up his head, coughed, and waved his hands in an effort to deplete the noxious smoke that swirled around him. "Let's just stick to the mission, Norbert," he hissed contemptuously. "And how about putting that thing out—you're not allowed to smoke in a subway car. What are you, crazy?"

"Since when?" Norbert purred, taking another drag. "I used to do it all the time. Christ, we smokers had our own separate train cars when I was alive. You know, people used to socialize back then. We'd share cigarettes and sales pitches. A smoking car was the place to be if you were traveling out of town. Those were the days. These damn kids today with their health degrees trying to push their beliefs on the rest of us. Look what good it's doing. Is *this* any better than getting lung cancer and dying?" He gestured to the cramped subway car. Every passenger was under the spell of his phone, head down, chin resting on ribcage, tiny headphones drowning out any threat of advancing outside noise or conversation, cocooned in a world virtual to the point of nonexistence. Only the very young and the very old looked around at the living specters that surrounded them, as outwardly lifeless and oblivious to their surroundings as the cold phantoms of Nox and Norbert riding on the bumpy car next to them.

•

"I don't know if this is something that my constituents are going to be interested in, Mr. Reese—"

"Reyes."

"Oh, yes. Sorry, Mr. Reyes. We're slowly improving our area using more natural and organic approaches to commerce. We have young families buying houses and fixing them up. We have upstart companies trying to bring back the main street. We have a booming pyrotechnics operation headquartered right here in Lawrence County. This area has already seen the crater that industry leaves when it ultimately packs up and finds a new home. There was a time when New Castle was one of the fastest-growing cities in the country, and then we lost so many families after World War II that it's taken almost this long to start seeing gains again. For a while there, we were just another stop along the rust belt here in the northeast. I don't know if the people of New Castle or the people in Lawrence County, for that matter, are going to be interested in playing host to the largest power plant that's ever been built. Why don't you try somewhere in Pittsburgh? We take things a little bit slower here in New Castle."

"Well, Mr. Pusky, I'm sorry to hear that you feel that way. It has been my pleasure meeting with you, and I do thank you so much for your time. I'll just leave this information here for you, and you can have your secretary get back to me when you'd like to reconvene. Feel free to run it by your county solicitors, council members, school board—anyone that you think might be interested in hearing about the many benefits that having our industry working with you and the people of New Castle would bring. I'll look forward to hearing from you." He paused, noticing a pennant hanging above Merrill Pusky's desk. "The Zips? You went to school in Akron?"

Merrill seemed shaken and then looked up to see what Nox was referring to. "Oh, that...yeah, no...I mean...my son goes there. Although, I think he spends more time partying that studying."

"Didn't we all?" Nox winked. "Well, that's my alma mater. Marketing with a minor in geology. Summa Cum Laude."

Merrill pursed his lips and nodded his head slowly.

Nox began advancing toward the door, and Merrill looked down at the pile of brochures and information that stuck out of the folder that the young man had left behind. He noticed something peculiar sticking out of the top of one of the pamphlets. "Mr. Reyes, I think you forgot something," he called out after Nox.

"Oh, no, no, no, Mr. Pusky. That's yours. Why don't you mull our little agreement over? Give it some thought. We'll be in touch, I'm sure."

He winked at Merrill and then walked confidently out the door.

Chapter 20

Like many aristocratic southern families, the Culpeppers descended from a line of English settlers who originally built homesteads in Virginia, but soon moved to warmer climates where the longer growing season meant that cash crops could be cultivated with greater success. On the backs of slaves, tiny seeds of cotton, sugar cane, and tobacco quickly grew into bushels of harvests and bounteous fortunes for the wealthy landowners. Instead of spreading the wealth with those who worked for them, larger barns were built to accommodate what was sown. Instead of sharing a space for all who toiled to bring food to the table, bigger dining rooms were constructed to showcase the opulence of the family to the occasional wealthy dinner guest of the Culpeppers. Even when slavery was abolished and the Culpepper plantation lost many of the slave laborers, sharecropping allowed them to continue much of their operation—and to keep their profits high.

After the turn of the 20th century, however, most of the Culpepper gentry had lost its fortune as industry and transit supplanted the increasingly unstable market for southern cotton and sugar cane. Using what was left of the money that they had from tobacco and the sale of the family plantation, the last three surviving Culpeppers sought out a new way of life and spread out throughout the south. Bixby Culpepper bought a small farm in South Carolina where he married, produced seven children, and successfully continued to grow tobacco—which experienced a boom in the post-World War II era. A recent Vanderbuilt graduate, Florence Culpepper moved to New Orleans. In the course of her long life, she would never marry after having lost her fiancée in the war, and she taught piano lessons and music at the McGhee school for girls before retiring after 40 years in the classroom. Being the youngest, Leroy Culpepper felt displaced and lost following the sale of the family homestead. He never liked farming as Bixby had, and he never went to school as Florence had. He had spent most of his youth in the stable, joking with the sharecroppers at dinnertime, or tending to the horses and going for long walks along the river.

After closing on the sale of the plantation, Bixby and Florence watched in fascination as Leroy walked over to the stable and began stroking the long, soft nose of Helios, his four-year-old Palomino stock horse. Without a word, he fitted a blanket and saddle onto the strong back of Helios, climbed aboard him taking only a canteen of water and the clothes that he had on his back, and set out down the long, dirt path of the overgrown plantation— allowing Helios to guide his course.

Over the years, Bixby and Florence would receive correspondence from all over. One letter came from as far west as a gold mine near Superstition Mountain in Arizona. A few years later, Florence got a postcard from the newly built Shrine of Saint Cabrini all the way up in New York City to show the girls at her school. Each message was the same: *Nothing feels like home yet. Helios and I are still looking.*

•

In the fall of 1957, the German U-Boats that had once surrounded Florida had gone, but the impact of World War II could still be felt in a burgeoning population. Fort Lauderdale had become a major Naval base, and business was booming. Ruddy, older, and tired of travel, Leroy Culpepper and his Horse Helios ambled onto a dirt path of a small town road just on the outskirts of the city. The main street had a dairy bar, a movie theatre, a laundromat, and at the far end, a funeral parlor that had been owned and operated by Bruno Berger and his wife Sonia. Sonia had passed away about twenty years earlier, and at his most recent doctor's visit, Bruno's physician informed him that he, too, had cancer and approximately three months to live.

"Daddy's not doing so well," Connie had lamented when a purring voice finally picked up on the other end of the phone.

"Not doing what well, Darling?" came the hum on the other end of the line. "Smiling? Showing compassion? Treating people with even a modicum of human decency?"

"I don't think he has very much longer, Norbert. Please come down." The line went dead, and Norbert listened to the loud, numbing tone for a minute before replacing the earpiece softly in its black cradle. He took a deep breath, reached into his jacket pocket, and took out a pack of Lucky Strikes. He removed a single match from the book that he kept by the table, struck it against the side, lit his cigarette, and inhaled deeply.

The following morning, Bruno's daughter drove into Fort Lauderdale from Pensacola where she had settled with her husband, an Admiral in the United States Navy. Bruno's son, Norbert, put the key for his rented bungalow in the Poconos inside a yellow envelope and left it with a check for $137.50 in the mailbox at the end of the driveway. He hopped in the waiting taxicab that would take him to the train station, and he said goodbye to the life of a traveling salesman that had taken him on a twenty-year venture from Florida to New York, then to New Jersey and into parts of Pennsylvania. He had been away for twenty-years—traveling, selling, moving—all of it just another way of hiding from a ghost he didn't want to face. And now, at the age of 37, he was coming home to the place where so many people literally spent their last days on Earth: preserved forever in the somber, quiet rooms of the family funeral parlor. Norbert closed his eyes as he bumped along in the jostling smoking car of the southbound *Orange Blossom Special.*

●

"This lady on my caseload's down in West Virginia, but I was thinking of taking a detour up past Pittsburgh. You don't mind, right, Norbert? I mean, she's a cashier at a dollar store—it's not like I'm going to be doing any magic for her or anything by trying to shift her day to positive. What's she going to do? Put an extra Snickers bar in some little kid's trick or treat bag or something? She's already got three positives anyway."

Norbert was barely listening. He was just sitting at his cubicle in the Expiation Zone. "Would you believe I've never been to Pittsburgh? Of course, I've never been in a dollar store either," he unenthusiastically replied.

"Hey, Pittsburgh it is, then! There's some unfinished business that I have up there—Solugrid stuff that I'd like to check into while I'm in the area, you know? Clean a few things up." Nox gave an uncomfortable laugh and kept trying to press the buttons on the uncharged cell phone that he was relieved to find in the back pocket of his black tuxedo pants. "I think there's a train that runs through Pittsburgh. We could catch that and probably still have time to do the mission if time permits and we're feeling up to it, huh, old man?"

Norbert looked at him out of his periphery and then rolled his eyes. He took a pack of cigarettes from his jacket pocket, tapped them against his other palm, and then waited to be whisked away. His mind was on something else.

Chapter 21

"You think this'll hold water, Chuck? I mean, we just need a majority vote from the council to change the zoning, and we can really get some wheels going under this thing."

"I'm not sure, Merrill. They just shot one of these down in Rhode Island, and they've had all that trouble over in northeast Pennsylvania. It's a different world that we're living in today. People are more informed than they've ever been, and there's a lot more transparency than there used to be. Every couple of weeks, a new politician is being brought up on corruption charges. You have to be careful with these kinds of undertakings, Merrill. Not to mention the red tape the EPA will put up. There's always a paper trail—no matter what they say. And do you really want this town to be the site of the largest one of these plants built to date? Are you sure that's a good idea?"

"Well, that's why I brought it over for you to look at, Chuck. I figured that if anyone would be able to point me in the right direction, it would be you. I'll just leave everything here on your desk, and you can call me next week or whenever you get around to it." He shook Chuck's hand and walked out the door.

"Merrill Pusky..." Charles muttered under his breath after Merrill had gone. He looked down the corridor, past the doorway through which Merrill had left. "When are you ever going to learn?" He shook his head slowly and then looked down at the brochures that his friend the commissioner had left on the coffee table in his office. Charles was about to throw them into the wastepaper basket next to his desk when something that was paperclipped to the top of one of the pamphlets caught his eye. Looking out the door to see that he was out of the line of sight of his secretary, Charles shoved the papers into a folder, and pushed them in a drawer in his desk.

•

Jennifer opened the drawers frantically. "Let's see what he's got in here," she said to Nox. "There must be a wedding ring, a wallet with some family pictures. I mean...this guy *does* have a family." She felt as if she was running out of time. "Come on, Buddy...this is your day! You only get five of these, and this is it. Don't do it! Do something right, Goddamn it!"

Nox looked at her, puzzled. He had never seen her this worked-up before. "Do you always tense up like this during a mission?" he asked, coming close and standing behind her. The two were in a motel room off the main thoroughfare outside Montgomery, Alabama, where Jennifer's fourth mission had only two remaining hours. "I think you should relax a little bit."

"I can't relax! You burned through half of my day trying to find out where the nearest train station was, remember? I told you there was no way to get to Pittsburg from here. It's ten at night for Pete's sake, and we haven't even seen this guy yet!"

"Take a breath," Nox continued, ignoring her. "Breathe…" He reached out and put his firm hand on her shoulder, but Jennifer tensed at his touch. She was furious that Patty had paired her up with Nox so that he could shadow one of her missions. He had almost sabotaged everything by trying to find a way to get from Alabama to Pittsburgh that didn't involve flying in a plane and wouldn't take too long. Between the late start and the extra trips to the metro station looking for maps, she had lost precious hours that she should have been spending on her case. "Let's go find Number Four. He went across the street." Nox pointed to the flickering neon lights on the road sign of the bar that was situated across the street from the motel. In the black of the night, the pink sign glowed, and the two non-functioning letters in the name on the sign emitted a slight sizzle—even though no light shone from within them anymore. From the façade of the brick building and through the screen door, live country music moseyed out into the warm Alabama night. "What do you say we join him for a drink? Come on, let's cross this bridge…"

Jennifer looked at Nox and sighed. As much as the thought of spending time with Nox in a bar revolted her, she knew that spending any more time out of the proximity of her fourth case would be a bad idea. Suddenly, she and Nox were inside the smoky, dimly lit bar across the street from the motel. Around them, she could hear the break of billiard balls, and the slow, even tap of the high-hat cymbals being played by the drummer of the live band. The blended sounds, colors, and sights of a bar five hours before closing time filled her with the sensation of what it felt like to be artificially alive. The couples who came in together at the start of the night were now cursing at one another and sitting on opposite ends of the bar, and the people who came in alone somehow found some stranger who filled in the empty aches in their souls after a few drinks. The captioned words of the muted sports commentators crawled in black and white along the bottom of the flat screen TV sets, the juke box blazed, and the bartender poured evenly while the tips got more generous, the music got louder, and the air got hazier as the evening staggered to an inebriated crescendo.

The song ended, and the two or three people who were still engaged and listening clapped and whistled through their teeth. At the break, the guitarist and the bassist stood facing one another and twisted the pegs on the ends of their guitars while the strings reached up, up, up, and found agreement with one another.

"Do you see him?" Jennifer whispered in a huff, trying to shake off the intoxication of the evening that surrounded her. "We're running out of time!"

Nox surveyed the length of the bar and saw where a middle-aged man was sitting at a high-top table with a woman leaning in unnecessarily close to him, pretending to be very interested in whatever he was saying. "Oh, yeah?" she asked, running a finger slowly around the rim of her martini glass. "How much longer are you going to be in town?"

"Just tonight," the man responded, blinking slowly. "I'll be heading home tomorrow once the crew is finished." He was slurring and had a hard time focusing on the words. The four glasses of whiskey that he'd thrown back to cut the sting of too many nights on the road had caught up to him and were hanging on tightly. He nodded and reeled closer to the woman.

"Target identified," Nox confirmed, pointing at the man with the glazed eyes and flushed face.

"Great," Jennifer exhaled dully, watching the woman giggle and move in closer toward him. "He's already half in the bag, and she's all over him! This is a lost cause." Sadness and disappointment filled her as she looked around the bar. Any of the potions and magic spells that she could have conjured to sway today to positive had already been whirled up, shaken, and blended together into the cacophonous and dangerous mix of a night out on the town far away from home. There was no reasoning with people once they had reached this point. She might as well face it: Mission four was going to be a loss.

Chapter 22

Norbert tilted his stiff neck toward one shoulder and then toward the other. He rubbed the base of his hairline where he felt the sore knot that had developed from sleeping poorly against the wall of the train car of the *Orange Blossom Special*. Looking over at the baggage claim area, he dug into his pocket and took out a crumpled pack of Lucky Strike cigarettes. There was only one smoke left. He put it between his lips, grabbed his two suitcases, and walked out of the train station and into the muggy Florida air. In September, the air in New York was already starting to turn crisp. The days were still long and warm, but the nights were becoming cool, and the leaves had already begun to fill the air with the pungent aroma of impending autumn.

Florida was different. The air outside was still just as warm as Norbert's blood temperature, and walking out of the train station and into the September air was just like wading knee-deep into a swamp. He was immediately sucked in.

Just off the platform, he was met with a slightly updated version of the town that he had left when he was seventeen years old. The events of World War II had changed a lot of aspects of the naval town, but there were some things that were familiar. The laundromat was still there, although the machines had changed considerably over the past twenty years, and he was happy to see that the ice cream shoppe that he used to frequent when he was a kid was still open and under the same management of the kindly German man who always used to give him an extra package of Lifesavers when he came in. He walked toward the country store and began to rub his eyes in disbelief as he got closer. "Lord above. Is that a *horse?*" he muttered to himself.

Norbert walked closer, and sure enough, a golden horse waited patiently outside the store, its long tail swishing and its radiant flesh involuntarily flicking as a fly landed softly and then was thrown off by the horse's deft movements. Norbert's eyes narrowed uncertainly, and he opened the creaky screen door of the general store.

"Well, I'll be damned," the older woman behind the counter of the store crowed as soon as she saw the slim build, neatly pressed suit, and the sparkling green eyes of the middle-aged man who had just entered the store. "First, I have a customer come riding in on a horse, and now a ghost walks in! Norbert Berger, is that you?"

"Hi, Elsie," Norbert purred. "I guess that old Nazi's not doing too well, huh?" Norbert had no interest in sifting through the small-talk to get to the heart of what the nosy proprietor of the general store wanted to know about his aging father.

"No, sir, he isn't," Elsie responded. "I haven't seen him in to get his coffee in about a week now. Your sister just got in. Seems like bad news, huh?"

"I suppose that depends on who you ask. What's the deal with the horse?" he asked, intentionally changing the subject about his father's health. "There's a damn horse outside, for Christ's sake."

"That's old Helios," a strange, southern voice broke in from across the aisle. "I've been riding him clear around the country for the past twenty-five years. We just got into town this morning, and that adamant ol' animal wont' take one more step without digging his hooves into the ground. I think my ol' palomino has finally found a place he wants to call home."

Norbert and Elsie looked at one another.

"Well, that makes one of us," Norbert purred after a moment. "Elsie, can I have three packs of Lucky Strikes, please?" He grabbed the cigarettes, left a dollar on the counter, and walked back into the muggy Florida air, eyeing the horse peculiarly, and then walking toward the end of the street as the screen door shut behind him. "Lord! I feel like I'm stuck in *Little House on the Prairie.*"

●

"You are the reason I've been waiting so long—some body holds the key," the vocalist sang into the thick, smoky night, her deep, sultry voice filling the air, silencing even the most stewed bar patrons and causing them to give pause and listen. The guitarist had swapped out his electric guitar for an acoustic one and was adroitly picking notes on the strings while the female singer belted out the final words of the chorus. Feeling disparaged, Jennifer took a deep breath and let the mesmerizing sound of the guitar and soft drums take her away for a moment.

"I'm near the end, and I just ain't got the time," the voice smoothly climbed. *"—and I'm wasted and I can't find my way home…"* The notes reached and improvised higher in harmony until the song came to a culmination amid the sound of more whistling and applause from the audience in the bar.

"Hey, you're not so bad," Nox praised.

Jennifer looked up, surprised, to see that he was talking to her. "What?"

"I heard you singing along. It was beautiful."

Jennifer had gotten so caught up in the song that she hadn't realized that she had been singing with it. A spontaneous smile crossed her lips. There was something about the last few years of her life that had come along and quietly shut the vent inside her where the music lived, and for the first time in a long time, she realized that it was now open again. She had forgotten how much she loved to sing.

"Seriously, Jennifer! That was really, really good." There was a genuine note in Nox's typically dubious demeanor.

"I'm a little rusty," Jennifer admitted, humbly.

"Well, you could have fooled me." For a brief instant, something sterling shone in Nox's dark eyes, and it stayed there for a moment while Jennifer held his gaze.

"Check, check," the lead singer intoned into the microphone, testing the sound and adjusting the volume on the sound board. "I think this one is in 'G,' boys," she said as the guitarist and bassist retuned their guitars, their notes filling the smoky bar with tentative, electronic scales until they reached unison.

Finally, the drummer clacked his sticks together three times, and the guitarist again began to nimbly pick at the strings. The patrons of the bar seemed entranced as the lead singer grabbed the microphone and began to sway and sing in her deep, soulful voice. After two verses, Jennifer began to sing along, and she was shocked to hear Nox pick up a harmony and sing with her. Her lead melody sustained the tonic note, and he filled in with a dominant pedal above it. "*Make me an angel that flies from Montgomery…just give me one thing, Lord, I can hold onto…*" Together, Jennifer and Nox filled the distance between the notes with natural intervals, and the progression between the two of them created a perfect concluding chord. "*To believe in this living is just a hard way…to…go…*" Together, each took turns holding a sustained note while the other danced around it as long as possible until they were both left breathless and the last of the drummer's soft cymbals faded.

The bar again erupted in applause and whistles while Jennifer looked at Nox speechlessly. "You? You sing?"

A mischievous half smile returned to Nox's face, and his dark eyes narrowed. "Well, not as good as you…"

Jennifer closed her eyes and inched her face closer to Nox. She drew in a breath from the air around her and for a brief moment savored the memory of what a night back on Earth felt like. Suddenly, the spell that she was under was broken by the crack of the cue against a newly racked set of billiard balls on the pool table behind her. She looked up suddenly at the

Genesee clock that hung behind the bar. It was 11:11. She had less than one hour remaining.

"Nox!" she commanded. "We have to get the hell out of here!"

Chapter 23

"This stuff is pretty strong!" Nox smiled, tilting back the glass and then shaking his head involuntarily. Beads of sweat were beginning to form above his brow, and he wiped at the mop of wavy black hair with the handkerchief that he had in his tuxedo pocket. "What do they call it?"

"It is a local wine," the bartender remarked slowly. "We have found that making our own is a better alternative to expensive, *foreign* imports." He smiled shrewdly and looked at Nox.

"Well, not all things *foreign* are bad. I think you'll find that Solugrid will—whew...that has a *bite* to it," Nox cringed, still shaking his head slightly. He was beginning to feel cold inside, though rivulets of sweat were now running down the side of his face. "Can I get a glass of water or something?" He began to breathe shallowly, and his eyelids felt heavy.

"My pleasure." The bartender looked across the ballroom at the Prime Minister of Georgia, who gave him a single nod, and then turned on his heel and walked away toward the balcony that overlooked the mountains. "This is what we call '*su*.' It's a mineral water that flows down from the mountains just outside the village. The locals collect it each day and truck it over to the hotels in the tourist district. Sometimes, it is carbonated so that the tourists can use it in their mixed drinks, but we locals find it is best to drink it cold and still, just the way that it is found in the natural spring. The natives of this region gather at the spring each morning to fill their own water buckets and bring them back to their villages. They use the water to keep their villages clean, cook their food, feed their children and babies...

"Water, Mr. Reyes, has always been a source of life here in the Anatolian region. These natives have relied on water for much longer than the Westerners have relied on oil." He focused his attention on Nox, who had begun to convulse involuntarily, and was swaying back and forth, trying to stay on his feet.

"Unfortunately," the bartender continued, "once infected...even the clearest and coldest of water cannot undo the damage that the poison has brought. So, the natives find it best..." he paused as he watched Nox collapse stone cold on the floor, "...to simply avoid what brings the poison."

•

"This stuff is pretty strong," David Pedwar mumbled as he stumbled with some difficulty back to the motel, leaning heavily against the blond woman whom he had met at the bar across the street. "Are you sure you want to do this?" he asked.

"I'm here, aren't I?" the woman responded, jabbing at him with her shoulder and then running her hands along David's jaw. She giggled and snapped her gum as she walked. Jennifer and Nox materialized behind them. Jennifer looked over at Nox, who was gazing intently at a card that he had taken from the pocket of the tuxedo jacket.

"What's up with you?" she asked.

"Nothing," he replied distantly. "Nothing at all…"

"Okay…" she rolled her eyes and continued following the man. She knew that there was nothing that she could physically do or say to stop David from giving into his desires. It was too late. Mission number four was a negative; she was simply going to have to accept it. "What are you staring at then?"

She tried to see what Nox was holding in his hand, but he made a fist and crumpled it when he saw her looking over at him.

David fumbled with the room key and eventually opened the door of the room, flicking on the yellow lights. "I'm just going to freshen up a bit," the woman proclaimed flirtatiously, leaving David and walking past the two full beds, and into the small bathroom at the end of the motel room. David began to take off his tie and unbutton his dress shirt as he watched the woman provocatively close the door.

"This…is…a…nightmare." Jennifer rubbed her eyes with both hands and then rubbed her forehead. Between the smoke, the stress, and the circumstances—she was developing her first postmortem headache.

"What exactly is the big deal, Jennifer? So you failed this jerk's stupid, arbitrary mission set up by Patty, the make-believe Queen of the Expiation Zone. What's so bad about that?" Nox jeered suddenly. "This is just some ludicrous game we're playing anyway. Don't worry. You can roll the dice and play again when your next turn comes around on family game night in purgatory. The Expiation Zone is a farce, Jennifer. It's a joke! *This* place is what matters. Earth. Where we are here and now. And you already lost it all here anyhow, right? I heard you sing tonight. You let go of whatever it was you were holding onto while you were here on Earth a long time ago. Something inside you was already dead, and you just didn't know it yet. As for me…I can still make things right here. *Here*! Instead, I'm wasting my time dicking around with these bozos and their problems because they all think they deserve to make it to Heaven. Well, you might have bought into the giant lie they've told you your whole life—and your whole death for that matter, but *I* didn't." He held out the crumpled card. "*This* is where it matters, not up there!"

Jennifer looked curiously at the card. *Nox Reyes, Account Executive of Acquisition, Solugrid Industries. Chicago, Pittsburgh, Helsinki.* Her brow furrowed as she looked from Nox down to the card.

"Solugrid…Pittsburgh…'make things right'? Wait a minute…I know what you've been doing. You blew those two missions that you were on last week because you've been trying to finish whatever business you had here with that insidious energy company you work for. That's a laugh—standing here saying that 'Earth' matters most to you when your career is spent catering to an industry that is slowly and systematically *destroying* it. Your time here is up, Nox. Accept it and move on."

"Those are some pretty big words for a hairdresser," Nox seethed. "What do you know about energy?"

Jennifer ignored him. "I knew it! I knew something felt wrong about this. Patty didn't put you up to this! You were just tagging along because you're desperate to find a way back to Solugrid headquarters." She advanced toward him with rage. "You're a worm, you know that? You *used* me to come back to Earth so you wouldn't have to use one of *your* days so you could get an extra crack at fixing whatever work you have left to do at your crooked job at Solugrid!"

"Yes, I did!" Nox exploded. "And so what? Did you have something better to do with your time? You screwed that up, too! You're just as much of a failure as that old crank Norbert—except you actually think you're doing something important as a Revelation 20, which just goes to show how *pathetic* you truly are."

Jennifer glared at him, and as her eyes narrowed, she focused on the glowing red numbers of the alarm clock on the bedside table. 11:49.

Jennifer turned away from Nox. "Norbert was twice the man that you are," she responded coolly. "If he wanted to, Norbert could close on a deal better than you ever could. And unlike you and your energy tycoon cronies, Norbert wasn't just smoke and mirrors..." Suddenly, the room began to fill with a thick, hazy cloud that made both Nox and David start to cough as each waved his hands by his face to try to waft away the noxious vapor.

Jennifer smiled genuinely in fond memory. "He was just..." The haze grew thicker. "Smoke."

PART III-JENNIFER

Chapter 24

The cough was incessant.

"I'm so sorry," David said, brushing past the surprised blond woman who had just come out of the bathroom door. The nag in his throat just would not go away. It reminded him of a time when he'd gone to church at Christmastime with his mom as a kid, and for some strange reason, he could not stop the steadfast cough that had taken root in his throat. His mom opened her purse and had given him a Luden's cherry lozenge. He held it on his tongue, under his tongue—nothing seemed to stop the cough. He clamped down hard with his teeth, eyes watering, as the ceaseless cough continued to knock at his clenched throat. He could feel the eyes of the pastor and the parishioners looking at him—some with worry, others with annoyance. *God, make it stop!*

His mom had escorted him to the back of the church where there was a little water fountain near where the Sunday school classes were taught, and he drank of the short, cool stream until his shoulders eventually stopped heaving and the coughing fit lessened, and he was finally able to breathe again.

David held his mouth beneath the tap of the motel bathroom faucet and began to drink in earnest.

"You okay in there?" came the strange voice from the other side of the bathroom door. In a moment of clarity that came from the cough and cold water, David's eyes narrowed with confusion at the unfamiliar voice, and then his heart sank. *What am I doing*? He coughed again, and his mind returned to the church of his childhood.

"What got into you, Dolly?" his mother asked with a smile once David's coughing had ceased. She leaned downward to look him in his eyes and rubbed his trembling shoulders.

David sniffed. "Let's just stay out here. I don't want to go back, okay?"

"Ok, Dolly. We'll stay. You don't have to go back if you don't want to."

David was ten then. A similar coughing fit would befall him seven years later, when he was in the quiet of a high school Physics room on an early Saturday morning, taking the SATs. Another memorable coughing spell would wrack his body on the day that his little girl was born. He had to excuse himself from the delivery room just before his wife was beginning the long, arduous contractions of active labor.

"Ahhhhhhhhhh!…" then three measured breaths. "Are you o—

aahhhhhhhhh!"

That was Anna. Patient Anna. Filled with iron.

"Something got me. I think it was that nurse's perfume. It smells like

that stuff they burn at church on Christmas. Are they even allowed to wear

perfume in hospitals anymore?"

Anna laughed. "I'm not sure. All I know is that if I coughed like that,

Emmie would be here by—aaaahhhhhhh!"

David smiled. "Should I get the nurse back in here? Nurse! Nurse!

Come back here with that nice, strong perfume of yours!"

"Stop!" She squeezed his hand.

Two hours later, Emmie arrived in a whirl of nurses, blood, and

quickly spoken jargon from the attending doctor, and towels, and beeps, and

then it all seemed to blur past in a cyclone through 20 years that began with

changing diapers, and then moved onto changing to a new company, and

then taking the position on the night shift, and then finding the traveling job

for the highway maintenance company that paid more and had a better

insurance plan. Then came the missed dance recitals, and the missed tea

parties, and before he knew it—missing Emmie because she had moved out into an apartment, and "Oh, hey, Dad...is Mom there?" Because it was Anna—it was always Anna holding everything together while he was out on the road, and Emmie had become a stranger to him. Just another stranger that he'd see over the hundreds and hundreds of miles.

Maybe that's where all the fire went at home. What passion was left to roar and blaze when Anna had always had to keep everything at a low simmer, trying to maintain some semblance of warmth as she waited for him on those late nights and lost weekends, all these years?

David shut off the tap and cleared his throat.

"You feeling better in there?" the coy voice flirted through the door.

"Not...not really," David apologized. "I think I'm going to turn in a bit early tonight. I'm...I'm sorry, ma'am. Really."

"Oh...okay..." The voice was tentative, hurt.

David listened for a moment until he heard the exterior door of the motel shut behind the woman. Then, he guardedly opened the door of the bathroom and crept over to the bed and crawled into it. He looked at the red digits on the motel alarm clock, and after a brief reluctance, dialed a one, then the area code, and then the seven digit number of home.

"Hello?" The voice was uncertain, and David detected fear.

"Anna? It's me. Anna, I just…I just wanted to hear your voice."

Anna looked at the green numbers on the clock next to her bedside table. 11:57 P.M. She rolled back onto her back and smiled. "Davey. How'd everything go today? I missed your call at dinner."

"Good…good…I was just thinking about that time in the delivery room with Emmie, and how I had that coughing fit," David laughed huskily, thinking about it with tears tugging at the corners of his eyes. "Do you remember that?"

On the other end of the line, Anna laughed. "That was twenty years ago. I'm surprised you remember that! I probably would have forgotten it forever if you hadn't said anything. Hey—are you alright? It's almost midnight, Davey. You get some sleep, okay? I'll see you in the morning, right?"

"Anna…I'm…I think I'm going to retire. I'm going to call my boss tomorrow and tell him I'm done working for the highway. I know Emmie's got two more years in school, but…I think we can swing it. I've put enough away over the years…and I—I love you, Anna. I love you so much, and I'm tired, and I just—I want to be home. With…" he broke down. "I just want to be home with you."

Tears welled up in Jennifer's eyes as she surveyed David and breathed a sigh of relief, watching his shoulders heave as he listened to Anna, dedicated, unyielding Anna, telling him that everything was going to be okay, and they would figure it out.

And he wouldn't have to go back if he didn't want to.

Chapter 25

"It was my fault," Jennifer admitted, stone-faced to the Head Intercessor. She looked over at Patty and Nox. "Please let her go. Patty had nothing to do with this."

Upon re-entry into the Expiation Zone, Nox and Jennifer had been immediately seized by the Board of Virtue. In bypassing the mission protocol, Nox had created a red-flag in the system, and now he, Jennifer, and Patricia were being detained in a holding chamber, awaiting trial for their breach of protocol and involvement in Jennifer's fourth mission. Jennifer and Nox's tablets had been confiscated, and even Nox's personal cell phone had been removed and was being held in impound.

"Sure, you'll stick up for *her*!" Nox snarled. "Why don't you tell her what you really wanted, Jennifer? Why don't you tell her about our *deal*?"

A man dressed as a sergeant restrained Nox, who was seething in one corner of the chamber, glaring at Jennifer. Jennifer swallowed hard and did not make eye contact with Nox. "I…" she stammered. "I—" Suddenly, tears began to stream down Jennifer's face. "I just wanted to know how I died, that's all. Nox said he could find a way to show me, and…" She slumped down, and Patty tried to move toward her, but she was stopped by another constable. "I'll take whatever the punishment is. I know it was wrong. I'm sorry."

"There you have it! Admission of guilt!" Nox sounded as he struggled against the sergeant who was holding him.

"I see." The Head Intercessor scrawled something into her tablet and then headed toward the door. "Raphael, Ch'eng Huang!" she called, "This case will continue tomorrow. I need you both to investigate the case files a bit further. I'd like you to audit the electronic tablets of Nox Reyes and Jennifer Uccello. I thought I'd never have much use for these new machines up here, but they might prove to be instrumental after all." She shut the door behind her without saying another word.

•

To: Jennifer Uccello (Jucce)

From: Ronald Montanari (RonMon521)

10:21PM

It was a pleasure meeting you this evening. I'll throw it out there, I find you very interesting and I can't wait to see you tomorrow. Bouna Notte, ron

"Excuse me, Your Most Eminent. I think I've found something.

•

The two sat at a high-top table just outside the little, corner restaurant, making small talk, drinking coffee and pointing out tidbits of the scene that was unfolding around them as they surveyed a world they had both experienced apart through a lens of unspoiled togetherness. Viewing what a stranger sees, discovering how they see it, and determining if it matches up with one's own viewpoint is the hallmark of any good first encounter. So far, things were going well.

A shiny green Jaguar convertible rolled slowly down the street in front of them, its fluid and arching lines commanding attention as its engine purred. "That must be a new model. I haven't seen one like that. He mustn't be from around here, that's for sure." They had been engaged in conversation for about 20 minutes, laughing and smiling, and sharing stories. It was the first time that either of them had truly laughed and smiled and felt comfortable in a long, long while. The conversation flowed naturally and without pause, fluidly coursing without running up against any large boulders of disagreement or falling into a silent cataract of contention. After so many days spent deliberately closing the door for self-preservation, maybe today would be the perfect day to unlock it and see what was out there. After all, everything that came before had come to an official end, so this had to be the start of something new.

"So…tell me about Helios, or whatever the hell you said his name was. Why on Earth would you want to spend all that time riding around on a goddamned horse?" Norbert asked.

Lee Culpepper smiled genuinely. "It's a long story," he admitted in his pleasant, southern drawl.

Norbert looked down the street and rolled his eyes. "Well, unless somebody croaks in the next half hour, I've got the time."

•

"Mrs. Uccello?" the Head Intercessor inquired as she looked Jennifer squarely in her brown eyes. "Does the name 'Ron Montanari mean anything to you?"

Jennifer thought back as far as she could. Her brain made a checklist of everyone that she had met since being in the Expiation Zone and of all the cases that she had had in her missions. Nothing there. She thought back to her time on Earth and tried to recall former clients, landlords, bosses, neighbors, schoolmates, friends. She was drawing a complete blank. She shook her head. "No," she affirmed, maintaining eye contact with the Head Intercessor. "No…I've…I've never heard of anyone named Ron Montanari before."

The Head Intercessor's cool blue eyes bored into Jennifer's for an extended moment. "Mrs. Uccello," the lofty voice of the Head Intercessor softened as Jennifer's big, brown eyes filled with tears. "Your Resident Guide, Patricia, has corroborated your story. And I believe her. You can return to the Expiation Zone and prepare for your fifth—and hopefully, your final—mission."

"Thank you," Jennifer whispered, breathing in coolly and deeply. She rubbed her temples with each hand, and her fingers instinctively went to the bare spot on her ear where her earrings once were. "Do I...?"

"All of your personal effects will be returned to you prior to your arrival in the Expiation Zone."

"Thank you," Jennifer whispered again.

"Jennifer," The Head Intercessor paused. "Before re-entry into the Expiation Zone, you will undergo a brief session with a pre-chosen operative. There's someone waiting to see you. It's procedural for all Revelation 20s prior to their fifth mission."

"Is it Ron Monta—whatever that name was?" Jennifer asked with a nervous laugh.

"No," The Head Intercessor replied succinctly. "It's your grandmother."

Chapter 26

Jennifer felt dizzy. And hot. The cool breath that entered and exited through her nostrils seemed to warm her, and for the first time in a very long time, every cell in Jennifer's body felt alive, and she felt every cell with atomic clarity. The circulatory system that once pumped blood, nutrients, and amino acids throughout her body now filled her with fire. And at a microscopic level, like the minute movement of a fly whose alighting from a flower results in an imperceptible dip in the petal, the tiny particles of Jennifer's being were beginning to change and flow as a result of fluctuations around her. She was being drawn to another unseen source of heat and light.

"Birdie?"

Tears immediately sprang to Jennifer's eyes, and she turned in the direction of the muffled sound. No one had called her that in ten years, and, though muted, the voice was just as she had remembered it as if she were hearing it from a bad recording.

"Birdie? Are you there?"

Jennifer moved toward the sound, and as she got closer, the room glowed brightly and became warm.

"Nona?" Jennifer called into the warmth. "Nona, can you see me?"

"I'm here, Birdie." Jennifer walked toward the end of a hallway, where she saw an oval mirror tacked up along the wall. She walked closer to the mirror, and she realized as she got nearer that it was not her own reflection, but the reflection of someone who looked very much like her. The lips were stained a matte crimson, and the auburn hair was twisted into pin-curls.

"Nona, is that...you?" Jennifer watched the smile brighten the face of the young woman in the mirror. She reached out to touch the face but was surprised to find her hand hit against the cool of the mirrored glass. "Nona! I want to see you!"

"I can see you, Birdie."

"I want to hold you," Jennifer cried, tears streaming down her face.

"Oh, Birdie...I want to hold you, too. I've wanted to hold you for the longest time." The mirror was, at best, like a projector. It took the energy of the operative and bounced it off the reflection of the initiate looking into it. If there were no mirrors, no cameras, no videos—if we never got to see ourselves, we could only hope that we could get a sense of our likeness from the way we are reflected and shone in the words and actions of others. A baby will instinctively stick her tongue out at someone sticking out his tongue. She will smile because she sees someone smiling at her. Chimpanzees will spontaneously imitate the actions of a human without any prompting. A couple once trained a harbor seal to speak in a Boston accent to attendees of the New England Aquarium. So much of what others do is simply a reflection of us being seen and experienced by them. Jennifer put her palm up to the cold glass, wanting to break through, but there was nothing tangible on the other side for her to feel.

"Let me look at you," Nona said, calming her. She looked intently and lovingly into Jennifer's eyes, and a smile spread across her face. "Some of my favorite days were when you were just a brand-new little baby. I wouldn't take my eyes off you, and I would just sit on the couch, holding you in my arms and watching you sleep all day. I used to think I could spend an eternity just snuggled next to you. Sometimes, I do…" She looked far away, and Jennifer was puzzled by what she meant.

"Do you remember that song your Papa used to sing all the time?" Nona's warm voice continued after a moment.

Jennifer pulled her hand away from the glass and smiled. She cleared her throat and sang softly and quietly, "Goodbye, Joe…me gotta go…me oh my oh…"

The warm voice chimed in. "My Yvonne, sweetest one, me oh my oh…"

Tears streamed down Jennifer's face, and she said the words hoarsely through her clenched mouth. "Dress in style, go hog wild me oh my oh. Son of a gun, we'll have big fun on the bayou." She covered her mouth to suppress her crying. She felt a warmness wrap around her.

"I remember when your Papa came home with a guitar one night and said he was going to play that song for me. Now, that man didn't know how to play a guitar any more than he knew how to take out an appendix, but he kept strumming and singing in time to that record all night long. He must have listened to that old Hank Williams song a thousand times, trying to get it right. About five in the morning, I came downstairs to tell him to turn the record player off because if I heard that song one more time, I was going to lose my mind. Well, didn't he turn around to face me in the dark of that parlor with the guitar in his hand, and play and sing that song for me in the pitch black without even looking down at the strings! 'I broke the needle on the record player about 3AM,' he said to me. 'It's just been me down here for the last two hours.' God, he sounded just like that radio…I thought that's what I was hearing…" The voice trailed off, and for a moment, Jennifer could feel in her Nona what she was feeling in herself. When we love someone;

when we truly love someone, something chemical happens. They become part of us, and when they go…the ache that replaces them is a cruel prosthetic to which we never grow accustomed. But…sometimes, we don't need to see them. Sometimes, we just need to listen. What we've been wanting to hear has actually been there, fused to us, the whole time.

•

"Everything that you love about what you'll see in that paradise of the Empire comes from what it was that you left on Earth, Birdie. We live for this outcome," Nona said, gesturing to something that Jennifer couldn't see. "Just about everyone wants to find Heaven or whatever paradise is waiting for them. Some of us spend our whole lives searching for paradise of some kind, and you might as well. What's the worst that could happen from living like you want to go to Heaven? But there's a point between where we start and where we wind up that's actually what's most beautiful. That tiny, little line segment is our life. Without our life on Earth, all of this would be for nothing." Again, Nona appeared to be looking off into the distance to a place that Jennifer couldn't see. "We could start in the Empire, you know. Some do. But most of us are on Earth for a reason. Everyone's got a bridge that they cross. Everyone's got to go to the river. The Empire, Heaven, Paradise, call it what you want—it consists of eternity…but Eternity…that consists of what you built with your time while you were on Earth. You lay the foundation brick by brick, stone by stone, little blade of grass by little blade of grass with what you did while you were alive. And that structure that you created is what you inhabit in eternity. *Ad ogni uccello, il proprio nido e il piu bello,* Birdie. There's no place like home. And yours will be the most beautiful of all—because it was made by you. As for the five days...well...isn't it nice to know that we are part of something so much bigger than all of us that we're all too small to see? Make the most of it, Birdie. You've got one more day. Don't just multiply that day by itself and keep it at one. See if you can do something for enough people that will make it hundreds. Make it millions. You'd be surprised at what one great thing can do. See if you can make it eternity."

Nona faded from the mirror, and her image was replaced by a hazy scene that cracked and blipped like an old home movie.

•

Irma. Day 3:

"I brought you a casserole, Mrs. Larsen." A young woman named Irma Pullman held out her arms and offered a floral pink Pyrex dish to her neighbor, Margaret, whose two boys had just been drafted from their home outside Chicago and were presently undergoing basic training for the Army at Fort Benning in Georgia.

"Oh, thank you, Irma," Mrs. Larsen said through sniffles. She blew her nose into her handkerchief and wiped the sides of each eye. She opened the door and motioned for Irma to come in. "You can just set that right on the table there, dear. I'm not worried about Francis—I know he'll do just fine." She blew her nose again. He's brave and strong, and he always does the right thing, but I worry about my Robert. He's so much more sensitive than his brother." Mrs. Larsen sank heavily onto one of the kitchen chairs and clasped both hands around her cup of tea, staring off into parlor where a painted picture of "The Last Supper" hung.

"I know, Mrs. Larsen," Irma said, pulling out another kitchen chair and sitting next to her.

"And just the other day, he came home from his milk route with this kitten that he said he found in the truck. I swear, that boy took that job with the delivery company just so he could ride around with these hapless animals he's always picking up…" Mrs. Larsen motioned to a crate filled with blankets on the floor. "And now that sensitive, young man is getting sent off to fight in the front lines. I guess I'll be stuck taking care of this cat now. Another mouth to feed…and with both my sons shipping out for that damned war…" Irma knelt down next to the crate and picked up the small, black kitten as Mrs. Larsen broke down and wept. It buzzed and buzzed as she scratched the velvety fur around its ears. "I told him to get rid of it!" Mrs. Larsen sobbed. "A black cat...that's the *last* thing I need right now."

"I can look after the kitten...if you'd like," Irma responded hopefully. "I'll take good care of him, and I'll write to Robert once a month to let him know how his cat is doing. Don't you worry, Mrs. Larsen," Irma promised, looking into Margaret's sad, tired eyes and drawing near to her. "I'll watch over this kitten...and...I think God is going to watch over Robert."

Despite Margaret Larsen's predictions and general likelihood, brave, robust, young Francis Larsen died in action during the Ardennes Counteroffensive later that year. Always much quieter and smaller, his younger brother, Robert, was selected for the armored division. He spent most of his days in the tiny tanks, proudly and dutifully serving under Lt. General George Patton, trying to drown out the noise of the bullets with peaceful thoughts and songs of home. He often fed his rations to the children and the animals that he encountered, and he kept pictures and letters in his helmet featuring his black cat, whom his neighborhood friend Irma Pullman had named "Tulsa." After the armistice, Robert Larsen returned to the quiet town of Riverwoods on the outskirts of Chicago, fixed up an old Buick that he could use on his milk deliveries, married Irma Pullman, and went to school on the G.I. Bill in the hopes of becoming a veterinarian someday. Robert and Irma would have no children, but they would always take in any strays that wandered the neighborhood, and they always had a house full of pets in need of a warm place to stay. Robert died peacefully of old age in his sleep—the war a far-off memory tucked deep in the recesses of his mind, folded up like the letters and purring cat pictures sent from Irma that he'd slip for safekeeping under the straps of his helmet, while the raging world outside thundered at war above him.

Chapter 27

"I know that lady!" Jennifer shouted excitedly, watching the scene that was presented on the mirror fade away to reveal the image of her grandmother again. "I've been to that town! I've been to Riverwoods, Nona! That was my first mission. Norbert and I saved her!"

"Yes, you did, Birdie," Nona smiled. "Isn't it beautiful?"

Jennifer thought about it, and a sense of melancholy tugged at her. She saved Irma, who had saved Tulsa the kitten, who had cheered up Robert and given him hope of coming home after his platoon had helped to liberate hundreds of thousands during World War II. He arrived back in the United States unscathed. She thought of her own home, the 'For Sale' sign in the yard, all fixed up for someone else to buy and enjoy. And then, there was just so much blackness. "No place like home" didn't feel the same when her home was no place. *Make it eternity,* Nona had said. "Who…?" Jennifer's eyes looked pleadingly into the eyes in the mirror. She watched as the image of her Nona gradually changed so that there was nothing remaining of her, and it was just a warm sensation surrounding Jennifer, who was looking deeply into her own sad reflected brown eyes.

"Who saves me?" she asked the cold mirror.

•

The two sat at a high-top table just outside the little, corner restaurant. "So…do you come here often?"

"I've never been here before, actually…I don't really get out all that much…I'm usually pretty tired after work, so I just go home and turn on Food Network and pretend I'm eating something nutritious instead of digging my fist into a box of Cheez-Its."

"I hear you there—hey, would you look at that!"

A shiny green Jaguar convertible raced down the street in front of them, its fluid and arching lines commanding attention before it disappeared in a roar down the strip. "That must be a new model. I haven't seen one like that. Are you into cars?"

"Into cars? Let's see…Maybe for the fifteen minutes that I'm *inside* mine before arriving at work and then for the fifteen minutes it takes to get back home. I don't even know what *year* my car is. I'm more into the songs playing on the radio than the actual car. So…no…I'm not really *into* cars, but my husband has—" She broke off. "I'm sorry…my *ex*…husband…"

"It's okay. We can talk about something else, but I like cars. Jaguars are quirky. Most European cars are. Personally, I've always had a thing for Italian cars…I thought with a last name like 'Uccello' that you would, too. I'm not really a Jaguar kind-of-guy. You just don't see a car like that all that often, that's all." There was something in the gentle, genuine response and the green eyes that allowed Jennifer to put down her guard—and wish that she knew even one thing—anything at all—about fast, Italian cars. *Another failure*, she thought, dismally. *My first blind date and I am blowing it!*

"Sorry…it just…takes some getting used to." Jennifer looked down and smoothed the material on her black "funeral" dress. She suddenly wished she had worn something else. Everything that she owned was black, and she was already feeling like the most boring person on Earth. On a whim, she agreed to sign up for an online dating service after talking with one of her clients who had just met the apparent man of her dreams through an app. Jennifer signed up that day and made an online connection with plans to meet after work that evening, and she was beginning to feel as if she had made a colossal mistake. *God, Jennifer*, she thought. *Would it have* killed *you to put on something bright and colorful for a change?*

As if sensing her thoughts, her date piped up, "That's a beautiful dress. It reminds me of one I saw this woman wearing in a play I saw last week."

"Well, now you're talking! What play was it? I hope it wasn't *Oklahoma* or something like that," Jennifer laughed. "Your profile didn't mention that you had an interest in theatre. Or, with a last name like 'Montanari,' do you only like *Italian* operas?"

"Now, it might be my turn to be awkward," her date smiled. "It was my daughter's play. It was a musical about personal hygiene…and my daughter was a floss fairy…but that dress…God, it was just like the one her piano teacher was wearing. It was very pretty…the dress…not the piano teacher…she's my neighbor, and she's, like 90…I'm not saying you look like you're 90! It's just…the dress…" Jennifer started to laugh as she watched her date turn red as a result of the deep verbal hole that he was digging.

"You are actually doing a really great job of being awkward right now," she smiled. "You're even better than I am."

"Thank you…I get lots of practice."

"So…tell me more about that play," Jennifer coaxed. "It sounds really interesting."

"Should I begin with the personal hygiene part?"

"Let's start with the daughter part," Jennifer reassured. "I liked that part."

"You...you did?"

"I think I'd like to hear more about it." She smiled genuinely as she watched the barrier that her date

had been putting up begin to crumble, revealing someone that she thought she would truly like to get to know.

"Well, her name is Audrey, and she's four. Hobbies include: Disney Junior, tea parties, and makeovers. Her mom and I have joint custody, so I still get to see her every day." Jennifer warmed as she saw the man come alive as he talked about his daughter. She was glad that she decided to keep an open mind and go through with the date. The two continued in conversation for two more hours, laughing and smiling. Jennifer had forgotten what it was like. For the first time in a long time, dinner had come and gone, and she had gotten through it without crying. Today would be a day to mark on the calendar.

"It's getting dark," Jennifer said, suddenly looking at the time on her phone. "I'm parked a few blocks over, so I'd better get going."

"I can walk you over to your car," he cut in. "I'd feel a lot better about it if you'd let me make sure you got there alright."

"I'll be fine. I think I'll still be able to tell which car's mine—even if I don't know anything about *Italian* vehicles," she smirked. "Besides, I don't know if I'm ready for that awkward moment where I have to get in the car, and you're still standing there, and I don't know whether I should shake your hand, or hug you, or just drive off without doing anything...so...let's just end today by me saying, 'I had a really great time this evening...and I'd like to see you again'...if...that works for you..."

He smiled genuinely. "I would actually really like that. Are you busy tomorrow?"

"Tomorrow?"

"I'd wait the standard two days, but that would take us to Thursday to ask you out again, and Thursday is 'Goat Yoga for Preschoolers.' Audrey's been working on her 'sun salutations,' and I'd like to make sure she's cool with everything before I introduce you to her...and her goat friends..."

"That sounds," there was a catch in Jennifer's throat. "That sounds...amazing. And, as much as I love the thought of goat yoga, I can wait a while to meet Audrey. That makes sense. But, let me know about tomorrow. Maybe we can find some Grand Prix to go to...or go skydiving or something. I've always wanted to do that." *Ugh,* skydiving, *Jennifer? Really? And don't act so desperate; you* sound like a teenager.

Ron smiled and watched Jennifer head down the block in the dim light of the streetlamps toward the direction of where her car was parked. He followed her with his eyes as far as he could until she rounded the corner and he couldn't see her anymore. There seemed to be a jubilance in her step, and he wasn't sure if it was her or the lights that were glowing. He smiled inwardly as he left several bills on the table and brought the check back inside and over to the counter to pay. Inside the noisy bustle of the restaurant, as the waitress handed him the printout for him to sign and return, he didn't hear the screech of the brakes two blocks over. He didn't hear the terrified cries of the onlookers or the horrible, resolute thud, and then the racing revving of the damaged engine. He was unaware that the ambulance siren, which sounded faintly in the distance of the city night as he walked back out the exterior doors to find his own car, was heading in the general direction of the restaurant, where two blocks away, Jennifer Uccello lay on ground, her cell phone glowing where it had been thrown ten feet from her, her body calmly splayed in the savasana pose, her spleen, kidneys, and gastrointestinal tract hemorrhaging internally as a result of blunt trauma, her heart pumping blood feverishly in a broken system, her brain already waking up in the blurry and disoriented white of the Expiation Zone as a crowd formed in the dark around her dainty, lifeless body on her last living day on Earth.

Chapter 28

Riiiiing. A phone sounded in the cavernous master bedroom of the Sewell residence. "Charles…" Rae Sewell moaned in her sleep and shook her husband's heavy arm. "Charles…the phone's ringing. Pick it up."

Riiiiing. "Huh…what is it, Raya?" He looked over at the gleaming green figures on the alarm clock next to him. "My God, it's 3:30 in the morning. Where are the kids?"

"They're in bed, for Christ's sake. Pick that damn phone up before you wake up the whole house. It's probably your great aunt calling in her sleep again…"

Riiiiing. "Hello, this is Charles," Charles barked tiredly into the phone.

A nervous voice chattered on the other end. "Chuck…Chuck, buddy…it's me…Merrill."

"Merrill…what the—what are you doing calling me at this hour?"

"Chuck…remember that favor you promised me a few years ago when I took you on as D.A.?"

Charles looked over at Rae to see if she was listening, but she had already fallen back asleep with her mouth wide open in anticipation of a snore. "Merrill, if this is about that plant and the money," he hissed. "I already told you—I think it's a bad idea…"

"I wish it were the Goddamned plant, Chuck," Merrill's voice cracked, and Charles could hear weeping on the other end of the line.

"Merrill, what the hell is going on here? It's three in the morning!" Charles barked into the receiver.

"That favor…" Merrill continued, composing himself. "I need you to make good on it, Chuck. I'm in a bit of a bind here…It's a bad one, Chuck."

"Are you at your office?" Charles gruffly barked into the phone, considering the time.

"No…I'm…home. I had to come home. Can you stop over my office this morning? How fast can you get here?"

"Give me a few hours. I'll be there as soon as I can."

•

Charles flipped through the files, witness testimony, and pictures contained in the police report.

"This is not good, Merrill."

"You're telling me, Chuck!"

"How's your wife taking it?" Charles asked, evenly.

"She's ready to go off the deep end herself. She's keeps saying it's all her fault—that she knew about the drinking and the drugs, and she didn't do anything about it. God almighty...we just bought him that car, too..."

"Hmmph..." Charles looked away from Merrill and flipped glumly through the pictures that were included in the folder. "Is that a cell phone?" he asked, squinting closely at an image in the dark corner of one of the grainy police photos and pointing to an eerie glow at the edge.

"I think so...it must be hers. They found it about ten feet from her, the poor thing. I think it's in a bag with some other stuff at the precinct." Merrill erupted into sobs again.

"Let me see if I can get a subpoena for the cell phone records of the victim. There was a case like this in California with regard to distracted driving," Charles said, rubbing his forehead.

"She wasn't the one driving, Chuck. The poor girl was on foot when he hit—" Merrill broke off again and tears flowed down his cheeks.

"I understand that, Merrill. Perhaps her *pedestrian* behavior was the problem," Charles stated, his voice level and unemotional.

Merrill looked at Charles with narrowed eyes. "You want to blame that girl for getting hit by a car, Chuck? My son was as high as a damned kite!"

"You want him to spend a few years in the cage for this, Merrill? You and I both know he'll never make it out of there alive once they found out who he is. The girl's already gone. We can't do anything to save her. Let me see if I can get those phone records. It's possible that your son could be exonerated—maybe even before this gets out of hand. He might not have to do any time at all…"

Merrill looked at Charles with bloodshot eyes. "You'd…do that? You think you can do that?"

"It's just one of the perks I've been privy to since you took me on as District Attorney, Merrill. Remember?"

Merrill looked down at the fragile, lifeless figure featured in the pictures, and an old pang resurfaced inside him. *She was someone's child, but*… his blood went cold suddenly. "Do it," he said resolutely. "Please. Do whatever you can to see if you can help my son."

•

"Lord God Almighty, it's starting to look like a drive-in movie around here! What the hell are you doing with all these cars, Lee?"

"Oh, I aim to fix 'em, then maybe sell 'em. I picked up a nice black Lincoln you might be interested in. She's only got 15,000 miles on her. Some front-end damage, though."

"You don't say…" Norbert cupped his hands around his mouth and lit a cigarette. "Tell me more."

"Well, she came in from across the state. It was a pretty bad accident, I guess. The lady driving hit a boy on a bike when he rode out in front of her. Poor little fella's probably never going to walk again, and the lady said she wouldn't get behind the wheel of another vehicle for as long as she lived, so I got it for next to nothing. I figure I could hammer out the big dent and shine up the rest. I'd sell it to you for about $200 if I could get it looking good again…unless you're spooked about the accident it was in. Some people get spooked."

"Darling, that doesn't bother me in the least. I'd be carting stiffs around in it anyway. Lord knows they're not particular." He exhaled some smoke into the warm Florida air.

"So you're gettin' used to the family business, are you? You seem to be keeping busy," Lee said, nodding in the direction of the building on the corner of the street ahead.

Norbert smiled, and his green eyes twinkled. "I've got job security here, Darling. Ponce de Leon might have discovered this place looking for that Goddamned fabled Fountain of Youth, but my phone rings just about every night to dig a new hole and add some fresh worm chow to it. Fountain, my foot! It's like I'm working on some assembly line like the ones they had up in the northeast, except I'm down here in cozy little Florida calcifying corpses. I'll let you know if I hit a spring for that fountain of youth the next time I'm digging a grave, Lee, if you think there's any truth to it. But God knows, you couldn't pay *me* to want to live forever."

"That right?" Lee wondered.

"Good Lord, no," Norbert said, taking another drag on his cigarette. "You think I'm smoking these cancer sticks for the health benefits? Get me outta here! And the sooner, the better, as far as I'm concerned."

"Well, I'm glad you're around," Lee said softly. He smiled. "Say," he changed the subject. "You ever been to New Orleans? I got a sister, Florence, living down there, and now that Helios is gone, may he rest in peace, I was thinking of going for a drive out to see her and visit for a few days. I could sure use the company," he looked earnestly at Norbert.

Norbert averted his gaze from Lee's. "Oh...I don't think so, Lee. I've got," he gestured his cigarette in the direction of the sign for the family funeral parlor. "I've got all this shit to deal with here. I couldn't...I couldn't get away and go traipsing off to New Orleans, for Christ's sake."

Lee nodded his head in understanding. He had been to enough places, seen enough people, and fixed up enough cars to know that sometimes there isn't a road long enough, a smile wide enough, or a paint thick enough to cover over a person's hidden dents of pain if the impact had hit them hard enough. Some people wall themselves in so well, there's no way of ever busting through. "I'll, uh..." Lee looked down at the dusty earth where his scuffed cowboy boots stood in sharp contrast to Norbert's shiny and well-oiled oxfords. Sometimes, two people could be standing next to one another in the same spot, on the same street, and still be living in different hemispheres. "I'll let you know if I ever get that car fixed up. She'd be perfect for you, I think."

"Yeah," Norbert purred. "Keep me in touch." Norbert walked back toward the funeral parlor, up the side ramp, and closed the door tightly behind him.

Chapter 29

"Patty?" Jennifer inquired hesitantly. She was waiting to review the dossier in her charging tablet in preparation for her last mission, and she came to the front desk of the Expiation Zone to ask Patty something that she had been wondering since she returned from her visit with her grandmother.

"What is it, Sugar?" Patty responded, not looking up from her files.

"Why did you want to become a Resident Guide instead of a Revelation 20?"

Patty looked up suddenly. "Girl, if I didn't have to die to get this job, I'd tell you I was born to do this! They picked me, Sugar! Didn't take too long before they approached me with the paperwork and asked if I'd be interested in a job like this—being here for people when they arrive and telling them what they can do to get to the Empire. I'm a natural people person, Miss Jennifer. Can't you tell?" Patty smiled broadly, but Jennifer noticed a sadness in her eyes. She ignored it and continued.

"You are," Jennifer agreed, shaking her head. "You're very good at it," she added afterward. "I'm glad that you were here to greet me when I…arrived." This was genuine. Patty's warmth was just the welcome that she needed, and Patty had done a good job of explaining everything to her so that she felt at home in this strange, barren place. She looked around at the stark white of the Expiation Zone. "Everything's just so white around here." Jennifer exclaimed, gesturing to the crisp walls and furniture that gleamed like snow around her. "You think they'd want to liven it up around here for when people first show up. Or is this not really the place for that sort of thing?"

Patty laughed heartily. "Yeah, 'livening it up' might be a conflict of interest. You don't want to give people the wrong idea, ain't that right, Sugar?" she smiled. "Then again, maybe that's why that asked me to be a Resident Guide. In a place white as this, I got enough color for everybody!" She shook her hips in emphasis, and Jennifer smiled. She looked down at her black dress and felt her diamond earrings in her ears, suddenly remembering something.

"Patty?"

"What is it, Sugar?"

"Did you know that my Nona was my Operative?"

"Your what, Sweetie?"

"My Operative. The Head Intercessor said that all Rev. 20s get a 'pre-chosen operative' before we go on our last mission. Did you know that my grandmother was going to be mine? Were you the one who chose her? Does it say that in one of the files that you have over there?" Jennifer asked, nodding in the direction of Patty's filing cabinet.

"No, Baby, I didn't choose your grandmother to be your operative, and I didn't know it was going to be her, but I might have guessed. She was listed as the person who made the biggest impact in your life, so it makes sense that she was the one you'd see before the fifth day. Usually, the person people see before their last mission is the person who meant the most to them when they were alive. I guess it helps to inspire them. God knows what He's doing, Sugar." Patty looked back down at her files and began sorting and organizing them.

"Uh huh…" Jennifer continued. "Patty?"

"What is it, Sugar?" Patty continued, still engrossed in her files.

"Did Norbert see anyone before his fifth day?"

"Oh, I imagine so, Sugar. All Revelation 20s get to, even that old misanthrope. Course, he probably met up with some tobacco sharecropper! Lord knows the only thing I ever seen him show attachment to was a cigarette. Wouldn't be surprised if the owner of the Lucky Strike franchise came down to pay Norbert a debt of gratitude for his patronage over all these years! Good God, that man could smoke! He reminded me of a cousin I had back in New Orleans…they used to call him 'Cool Hands'…" Jennifer wandered away and kept Patty to continue her lengthy history of her family back home.

•

"I'm supposed to just wait here like this? I wouldn't be surprised if the Wicked Queen showed up with a box to stick a young maiden's heart in and asked who the fairest one of all was! Well, whoever it is, I hope they keep it brief. There's nobody that I feel like having a conversation with right about now anyhow."

Norbert waited and looked at the stark white walls around the mirror. He tried to focus on everything but the reflection that stared back at him. Eventually, he gave in, and he inspected the deep wrinkles that lined his mouth and eyes—the usually sparkling green eyes that now appeared uncertain and ancient in the mirror. He looked at the wild yellow of the fake hairpiece and then at the wiry gray of the natural hair that peeked out from underneath. What was it that he was always trying to cover over and hide? "Alright, already!" he entreated to the reflection. "Bring whoever it is in! I don't have all day to wait for whatever is coming to see me…of course, I'd be stuck with some last-minute poltergeist with no regard for punctuality…come on out, for Christ sakes!"

Norbert watched the anger slowly fade from the person making demands in the mirror, but it was still just him…waiting.

•

"Good morning, Elsie," Norbert purred, as he placed a coffee cup and a roll of Life Savers on the front counter of the general store. "My usual, please." Elsie took three packs of Lucky Strikes from the wall behind the counter and placed them in a stack next to Norbert's coffee and Life Savers.

"How's your buddy doing?" Elsie asked. "I haven't seen him in here in a while."

"What buddy would that be, my dear?" Norbert buzzed. "You'll have to be more specific. You know I have so many associates around here in this bustling, social metropolis—chock full of congenial neighbors and friends," he smirked with mock boastfulness and gestured to the main street scene outside the large front window of the general store where three men stood talking outside in the parking lot. "I couldn't possibly tell the specific person who whom you are referring when you make a generalization like that."

"My mistake," Elsie scoffed. "I thought you were friendly with that southern fellow who's been fixing the cars in town. I've seen the two of you eating lunch together before. You know, I've been wanting to have him take a look at my car, but I haven't seen him in a few days. It's making a noise."

"Might just be you," Norbert snorted, under his breath. "You and your infernal gossip make enough noise for all of us here in town."

"I beg your pardon, Norbert? You're going to have to speak up if you want people to hear you."

"Oh, it was nothing, Darling." Norbert placed two bills on the counter, grabbed his cigarettes, coffee, and Life Savers, and walked out the door of the general store, his exit clanking the little bell as he strode back across the street and into the humidity of the muggy Florida morning.

"Lord, he has turned quite strange over the years. He's not the way I remember him to be when he left as a young man, that's for sure." Elsie muttered.

"Well, you know his father always said that he was a queer one," a gruff, male voice spoke from behind the rack where the penny candies were held.

"That is true," Elsie said, shaking her head. "Course, old Mr. Berger, Sr. didn't have too many nice things to say about anybody. It's a good thing that family stuck with the dead instead of the living."

"Sure is," agreed the voice. "Sure is."

•

Norbert waited, staring at the figure in the mirror. He inspected the knot of his tie in the mirror and decided that it needed adjusting. He undid the horseshoe tie clip and began to loosen the knot around his throat.

"I can't believe you still have that," a warm, Southern voice sounded from around him.

"The throat or the tie pin?" Norbert purred, not looking up from his work. When he finished, a cursory glance in the mirror still revealed only himself. He felt a warmth, but he couldn't tell the direction from which it was coming. "Either way is shocking, I guess." He looked down again and continued to unknot and retie his necktie. "I'm not exactly sure why it is that I've held onto it for so long, it's as tacky as hell."

"I guess so," the voice continued. Norbert searched the mirror, but only his green eyes returned the imploring gaze.

"I don't really have much to say except I'm sorry," the faceless voice danced around him. "If I'd a known I wasn't going to see you again, I don't know if I would have just up and left the way that I did. I don't know if I would have left at all."

"That was a long time ago," Norbert responded to his own face in the mirror. "It was a different time then." He gave one last look in the mirror, but he was still greeted by his own reflection. "I've laid out and buried a lot of people," Norbert continued, looking into the sparkling green eyes. "I've heard a lot of people say their last goodbyes to a lot of other people who had no idea what they hell they were saying because they were dead and lying in a casket. Just like us two schmucks are now," a smile curled at the edges of Norbert's lips, and his green eyes glimmered in the mirror. "You know, I've been here doing what you might call 'living' through whatever this is for almost 30 years, and I still don't believe in any of this shit I've seen up here."

"You're not living," the southern voice reminded him.

"Hmmph," Norbert purred, lighting up a cigarette. "If that's not the damned truth..."

"But *they* are," the voice continued. Norbert looked earnestly at the mirror, but still only saw his face as the exhaled smoke swirled around it. "Whether you believe in any of this or not, they're livin' down there," the southern voice continued. Norbert rubbed his eyes and his temples vigorously. "And one of them might need you. And maybe...maybe you need one of them."

"Hhmph."

You've got one more day," the voice reminded him. "Whyn't you try to find a place that feels like home to you. I can't imagine it's where you are now. You'll know it when you're there, I promise. But, you and I both know it's not hiding out in here. She needs you, Norbert."

"Yeah…? Well…"

"You need her, too."

Norbert stared into the cold mirror.

Chapter 30

Hell is cold.

It shocks you like a winter morning

Sneaking in your early door

And it chills you with no warning

Freezing you through to your core.

You'll search for fire to escape

The ice entombing your bare skin

But nothing warm is found here

In the lonely depths you're stuck within—

Hell is cold.

Hell is you.

It's every sin and wrong you've done

Revealed to all and then returned.

And all the inner corruption

Flails against the fate you've earned.

For lifetimes you suffer, seeing

What was missing in your errant soul

And this tormented state of being

Is but a single hour's toll.

Hell is you.

And when there's nothing left of you

And the Hell that you've become,

You crawl inside all that you knew

And hide there—

Wishing you were numb.

'Cause ice and fire both feel the same

If it's cold or hot enough

That tear shed for your old, old flame

Reminding you

that Hell is hot.

"Patty…! Patty, what the hell is this…?"

•

"I have never seen anything like that before. Good Lord, these new machines are more trouble than they're worth. Where'd you find that miserable excuse for literature, Sugar? 'Hell is cold,' my foot!" Patty stared, wide-eyed at the poem that illuminated the screen of Jennifer's tablet.

"I turned on the power, and…it was just—there! On my screen. On my tablet. As soon as I opened it--" Jennifer was breathing heavily, and her shoulders shook with each cold breath. "Who would do this to me? What does it mean?"

Patty put an arm around Jennifer. "Baby, I don't have the faintest idea who sent this to you or where it even might have come from. Good Lord, I never thought I would live—or die—to see the day that hackers would start sending hate mail in the form of poetry to the poor people waiting for redemption in the afterlife! Still, I would not let this get you down, Miss Jennifer. I don't think this message means anything—maybe it was just some crazy kids pulling a prank or something. You know how people can be! I've reviewed your files, and you have had four positives in record time. Do you know how difficult it is to do that? Maybe it's just somebody here in the Expiation Zone feeling a little jealous, that's all. You just pay no mind to that whatsoever, you understand me, Sugar? You just focus on this fifth mission of yours, Miss Jennifer. I knew from the start you were destined for good things, and I still feel that way. It's not Hell. I promise you that, Sugar. It's not Hell you're destined for—the good Lord knows that."

Jennifer sniffed and wiped a stream of tears from each eye. "I'm ready for my mission," she vowed, suddenly determined. "I'm ready to leave. I'll..." she looked deeply into Patty's eyes. "Wait—am I ever going to see you again?" she interrupted herself.

Patty smiled wordlessly, and then shook her head. "That depends on a lot of things, Miss Jennifer. A lot of things," she answered after a moment. "But...if I had to guess," she took Jennifer's hand in hers and laced her warm brown fingers with Jennifer's thin white ones and held tightly. "I think it might be a while before you and I see one another once this mission is over.

Like I tol' you when you arrived here, Sugar, my mama always used to say that nobody ever comes back to tell us what happens when they die. And we are all just energy that needs to go someplace. When you first came, I tol' you that my place was probably different from yours, but—" Patty sniffed back the sadness that had overcome her, and she smiled broadly at Jennifer. "But…I hope there's someone like you waiting for me when my shift here is over and I get to wherever I'm going. I wouldn't mind being welcomed by a heart like yours when I get home, that's for sure." Jennifer's eyes began to tear, but she found strength in the tender and proud face that looked back at her. "But I am telling you now, Sugar, you've got to let go to fly sometimes to find what it is you were destined for. You are filled with more good energy than I've ever seen. But, you've got to…let go…to fly." Patty squeezed Jennifer's fingers one final time, and then released her into her fifth mission.

●

"Bonnie, see if you could get Terry down at the station on the phone for me, will ya?" Charles Sewell pushed a button on his desk phone, and then returned the earpiece to the cradle. He rubbed his temples and then ran his hands along the side of his graying head. At that moment, his cell phone began to ring and vibrate in his pants pocket. "Jesus Christ," he mumbled. "Hello?" he snarled into the phone.

"Did you hear anything yet, Chuck?" a frantic voice on the other end asked.

"Nothing official, but I think we're going to be just fine. Let me call you back in an hour or two, okay, Merrill? I've got to go out and meet some people for lunch, okay? Let me call you back in a few hours." Charles pushed the button on his phone and resumed rubbing his temples. "God Almighty! Bonnie! Bonnie!" he called out to where the secretary sat at her desk just outside his office doors. He rose from his leather office chair, grabbed his wallet from his desk, and walked out the door of his office and toward her. "Bonnie," he said, more quietly and calmly this time as he reached the desk of the salt and pepper-haired woman, who sat knitting a scarf, completely oblivious to the fact that he had been calling out to her. She looked up and made eye contact with him and smiled. "Hi, Chuckie! Do you like this scarf? It's for little Lucas. Won't he look so cute in it?"

"It's beautiful, Bonnie. Just the sort of thing you should be working on right now instead of compiling the case history for our presentation to the zoning officer and town council later this afternoon."

"Hmmmm?" Bonnie responded in confusion, looking back down at her knitting needles.

Charles heaved a sigh and took his rain jacket from the coatrack next to Bonnie's desk. "I'm going to meet with some people from the Chamber for lunch. Could you let me know if anyone from the precinct stops by? I've been expecting someone—nothing important, but just let me know if anyone from downtown comes by while I'm out. And...if you get a minute," he said, looking down at the scarf, "could you prepare those files for me?"

"Yes, *sir*," Bonnie replied, looking back down at her scarf and smiling at her nephew Charles. He grudgingly returned the smile and then walked out the door.

•

Jennifer left Bonnie and followed the man down the corridor of the hallway with her eyes, and then she went into his office. In the dim light that filtered in through the blinds, she stood over the highbacked leather chair and tapped against its side, causing it to spin around like a slow-moving roulette wheel. She watched it spin for a moment, and then walked over to the filing cabinets. Her study of the information that had been provided in the electronic dossier only supplied her with a cursory understanding of the details of her fifth mission. Apparently, Charles Sewell was 58 years of age, had one son from a previous marriage and was married a second time with two more daughters.

The physical description in the tablet listed salt and pepper hair. Gray eyes. Bonnie Sewell, aged 75, was a great-aunt, related through marriage, who had been working for Charles ever since her husband had passed away when he was a young man. Charles never had the heart to let her go. He had attended Penn State and then earned a juris doctorate from Phoenix School of Law. He narrowly passed the Pennsylvania Bar Exam, and he had been practicing as a lawyer since the late 1990s. He had become District Attorney of the small area outside Pittsburgh about three years ago, and Bonnie followed him there to stay on as his secretary—always proud of his accomplishments. Jennifer looked up on the wall where the framed diplomas from both institutions hung. "Well, that checks out," Jennifer confirmed to no one in particular. "What else is there to know about the Sewells? You're teetering on the edge of something momentous here with two negatives and two positives—and, from the looks of it, not much time left. Help me hit this walk-off homerun. No pressure..."

Jennifer circled back over to Charles Sewell's desk. She saw a framed picture of a young man who appeared to be just a few years younger than she herself was now. He wore a graduation cap and gown and was smiling as he held up a rolled diploma. Next to that frame, two grinning girls with missing front teeth smiled from beneath giant bows in the acrylic bases of old school pictures. Behind them, an older, middle aged man with graying hair stood framed next to a buxom, middle-aged woman with short, red hair who was holding a large fish that she must have just caught on the end of a hook. Jennifer smiled at the wide, surprised, but charismatic grin of the red-haired woman wielding the giant fish in the picture.

Her gaze was suddenly drawn down to the desk where a manila folder sat splayed across the blotter with the word "CONFIDENTIAL" stamped across it in red ink. Her smile faded, and her brows knit together in confused concern as she read the name that had been written in blue pen across the tab on the front of the folder.

Jennifer Uccello

Baffled, she picked up the folder and opened it. Her eyes scanned across the first of a series of glossy and gruesome photographs that had been paperclipped together. She undid the paperclip and flipped through the pictures. Each one showed an image of a slender, young woman with dark brown hair, lying lifelessly on a dimly lit street. She was wearing a form-fitting black dress, and her eyes were closed. Small diamond studs glittered in each ear. Every photograph revealed a different angle of the scene, and with every angle, the terrible truth became clearer. The impact of what she was seeing struck her with a stunning force, and for the second time now, her delicate body crumped breathlessly to the ground.

Chapter 31

There is an Iroquois legend in which twins are born to the Sky Woman. Some tribes say these twins were day and night. Some say the right-handed twin was born normally, but the left-handed twin was born of the Sky Woman's side and killed her. Some say the twins represented summer and winter. Life and death. Some say these twins are good and evil and that they brought both traits to the world with them when they came, and that's why people just are the way that they are. Some say the good twin defeated the bad twin and sent him to live in the underworld forever. Some say the evil one is the one who prevailed. Maybe it is all just to prove that there are two sides to every story—even ones old enough to be about creation itself.

●

"Do you want to talk about your brother?"

The clock on the desk ticked loudly.

"Stephen, I was looking over your files, and I have some questions for you. Would you feel comfortable telling me about your brother?" the doctor repeated softly.

"No."

The clock on the desk continued to punctuate the silence of the room.

•

"Hey! Give me that!"

Two boys rolled on the ground, fighting over the shining silver robot toy with the gleaming rectangular chest that the smaller one held in his fist. "It's mine, Stephen! You have your own," the smaller one called out from under the pin of the larger one.

"Fine, take it!" Stephen threw the toy across the room. "I don't want your stupid robot anyway. I'll probably get cancer cooties from it," the young boy snarled.

"Hey," Toby said, standing up and looking at his brother. "That's not nice."

"You boys had better be behaving in there!" their mother called from the kitchen.

"We are!" they said in unison.

"Mom said you can't get cancer from me," Toby continued in a whisper, looking earnestly at his brother.

"Well, what would *she* know?" Stephen jeered. "She's not a *doctor*."

"I *asked* the doctor. I asked him after all the kids at school stopped sitting next to me at lunch when my hair started falling out after my last treatment. He said people can't catch cancer from me. And I asked him if you were going to catch it, too, since we're twins and he said you wouldn't. I *asked* him, Stephen. I *asked* him." Toby looked up at his brother with big, wet brown eyes.

"Well, did you ask him if cancer is the reason you're such a dweeb?" Stephen smiled in mock-contempt. He jabbed his brother in the arm. "'Cause I don't want to become a dweeb if that's contagious...since you're my twin and all."

Toby smiled lovingly at his brother, and the two resumed playing, pretending they were robots on the rug of the toy room.

●

"Have there been any changes since we met last week?"

The clock continued ticking in the silence of the room.

"Stephen, for the entirety of our last two sessions, you didn't utter a single syllable. I'm beginning to feel a little guilty about taking your copays if you're just going to sit in the room and wait until the hour is over. I want to help you. I understand that the court has appointed you to be here, but I think it would be worthwhile for your therapy if—"

"Aren't you just another crony taking money from my father and making sure I don't go to jail for what I did?" Stephen grumbled, interrupting her sullenly. "What do you care?"

The slim black woman rose from her chair and walked over to the window of the small room.

"The brain is a remarkable thing, Stephen, and developmental traumatology has revealed that there are lifelong repercussions for people who have been exposed to significant stress during their youth. What happens to us when we are children stays with us for a long time—even if it isn't medically categorized as pediatric trauma," she said, staring out the window. "When I was in second grade, our teacher had us all trace our hands to make a Thanksgiving turkey out of them. We were supposed to take our tracings home, decorate the fingers with feathers and glitter, and then bring them back to hang up on the bulletin board. I considered myself an artist back then. I didn't want to make a turkey out of my hand. I wanted to take my little, brown hand and finally make it look pretty, so I took the peach crayon out of my big box of 64 perfectly sharpened Crayola crayons, and I colored my fingers so that they looked like the hands of the other white girls in my class. Then, I drew a big diamond on the ring finger, and colored gold rings on every other finger on the hand—even the thumb! I took out my mother's nail polish and gave my hand long, red fingernails that didn't look stubby and bitten down like mine were in real life," the doctor exhaled and continued. "When I came back into the classroom the next day with my hand, proudly waving it at my second-grade teacher, she took one look at it and threw it in the garbage can in the front of the room. She accused me of stealing one of the other girl's drawings and trying to turn it in as my own. I guess she might have been mad that I didn't follow her directions and make one of those hideous hand-turkeys. Or maybe she just didn't believe that a little girl with chewed-up fingernails and brown skin could have made something that looked even remotely pretty.

"That day was over forty years ago, and I still remember the pain, the embarrassment, and the anger of that singular event like it was yesterday. You have a history of substance abuse, Stephen. The most recent incident of which has allegedly conspired in the death of a young woman. I am interested in seeing if we can identify a starting place in your biological stress system so that we might be able to work toward an ending place in your cycle of addiction. I don't personally know your father, and I am not one of his 'cronies,' but I would like to offer you the therapy that you most certainly need and to try to keep you out of jail if I can."

"Well, good for you, lady. That was a nice story. Here's a hand for you," he raised his middle finger in the air, smiled at her, and snarled, "Good luck fixing me. Nothing ever has."

"Do you want to talk about your brother?"

"No."

The clock ticked.

•

A cold wind whistled through the barren trees of the cemetery. Stephen looked around at the black coat bottoms, black pants, and black shoes that surrounded him. He scratched at the neck of his new, crisply ironed shirt under his jacket collar. He did not like this new shirt at all.

"O God, all that you have given us is yours," the pastor intoned, mechanically.

"Mom?" Stephen pulled on the sleeve of his mother's black fur coat.

"Not now, honey," Stephen's mother whispered, wiping the corners of her eyes with a handkerchief.

"As first you gave Tobias Jason Pusky to us, now we give Tobias back to you." The pastor put his hands on the small, rectangular polished coffin and continued, "Receive Tobias Jason Pusky into the arms of your mercy. Raise Tobias up with all your people—"

"Mom—"

"Not *now*, Stephen!"

"Receive us also, and raise us into a new life," the pastor continued in a monotonous tone.

Stephen crept slowly away from the large group of mourners, unnoticed, and ran as fast as he could down the street and away from the cemetery with the talking-robot pastor, and the cold, gleaming silver box with his twin brother locked inside it. Once he was out of breath, he slowed to a walk and unzipped his jacket, itching the spot where the starched collar met his neck. He tore at the fake clip-on tie and the buttons on the front of his shirt so that it fit loosely and comfortably around his neck and didn't scratch anymore. Then he stuffed his cold and red hands inside his pockets where his little fist met against the rectangular chest of the small toy robot that he forgot to put in the casket with Toby in case he wanted to come out and play later. He looked back in the direction of the cemetery, where his cousins, aunts, uncles, mom and dad still swarmed around Toby, and he started walking back toward them with the toy held tightly in his hand. He wanted them to open that terrible box up and wake up Toby. In case he wanted to come back out and play.

Chapter 32

"This will require a zoning change, Mr. Sewell," the man said, handing the file back to Charles, and taking a sip from his glass. "That means it has to be brought up publicly. After tonight, we won't meet again for another month, and that's simply not enough time to do the third-party research that this sort of undertaking requires. Let's table this for the time being. It's not a good idea to pass a project of this magnitude too hastily without giving it due diligence."

"I don't know, Bob," another woman said. "I'm sure Chuck can pull a few strings. This town's been in a slump for years, and this might be just the shot in the arm that this area needs to improve commerce. That's how we'll pitch it to 'em, right Chuck? Hit 'em in the pocket. I think the public will warm up to the idea once they hear the benefits."

"The proposed—and rather dubious jobs—are not sustainable," Bob interrupted, pointing to the file in Charles's hand. "We're looking at a few dozen union positions that would be on site for 18 to 24 months, max. There's nothing permanent. There's certainly nothing here for your average local resident currently living in the area. And think of the wear and tear of those construction vehicles on the roads. Our budget is already through the roof on road repair, and we just put in that new sewage system."

"I just need the board to see if we can label this project so that it falls under 'permitted use' instead of 'conditional use,' that's all—" Charles broke in. "With permitted use, this wouldn't even need public approval—or knowledge. We just have it put in front of a zoning officer for a signature. The council doesn't even really need to know about it."

"I don't like the sound of that, Chuck," Bob said, wiping his mouth with a white napkin and then throwing it on the table. "People are going to find out about this. They're going to want answers once they see all of the equipment rolling in and the land being cleared."

"Bob, you don't have any vision," the woman continued, dipping a french fry in ketchup and continuing to talk with a full mouth. "Besides, people don't know what they want. Let Chuck see what he can do. Have him talk to Merrill. Say, how is Merrill? I heard his son was in an accident on his way back to college last month. How is—what was his name, Chuck? Shane? Something like that?"

"Stephen...his name's Stephen. He's doing...alright...poor kid. A lady...walked right out in front of him."

"Oh dear!" the woman said. "How awful! Well, tell him we said we hope he gets well soon. God Almighty...some kook walks out in front of him, and now the poor kid has to deal with the consequences for the rest of his life...the nerve of some people! And, Chuck, don't wait too long on this Solugrid deal. I think it would be a real win for our area. I think the locals would like it once they saw what it would do for the economy. See if you can file it under 'permitted use.'" She grabbed more fries and smeared the red across her plate with them before taking a greedy bite.

·

Mom and Dad,

The therapy isn't working. I don't know if you could ever know what I'm going through right now.

Stephen took a drink from the can of beer he held in his hand and reached in his pocket. He took out the bottle of pills that he swiped from his roommate's gym bag earlier that day and placed it on the cold, white porcelain of the sink before looking in the mirror at his haggard reflection and taking another long drink.

I've tried for years to numb the pain, but I can't hide anymore. And this last thing...well—

Stephen drained the can, and then produced a small plastic bag from the medicine cabinet. His racing mind returned to the night of the accident a few weeks ago. He was driving from Pittsburgh back to college in Akron after a botched weekend at his hometown when he decided to pay a visit to his old dealer in Youngstown. He had been clean for almost two weeks before he walked back into the doors of his childhood home.

•

"Mom!" he called out into the darkness, closing the heavy, etched glass door behind him. Stephen set his duffle bag and another bag of laundry down on the tile floor. "Dad?" he called out into the open foyer, his voice echoing off the walls. Trusty, their ancient beagle, slowly rose from his dog bed and sauntered over to Stephen. "Hey, buddy," Stephen said, bending down to scratch behind Trusty's ears. "It's nice to know *someone* around here is glad to see me." Trusty rested his gray muzzle on Stephen's leg, and a wet spot of drool began to form on Stephen's jeans. "Ewww…Trusty!" Stephen said, laughing in spite of himself.

•

"Touch it!"

"No, you touch it!" Toby shot back at his brother, who was holding his finger and forcing his wrist closer to the dog's slimy mouth. "I don't want to touch it!"

"For five bucks, I'll do it," Stephen said, dropping Toby's arm and smiling at him.

"I only have two dollars left," Toby said. "I gave you three dollars when the ice cream truck came yesterday, remember?"

"Well, that's too bad," Stephen said. He walked over to the sleeping puppy, wiped his hands along its dripping jowls, and then proceeded to smear the sticky goo all over Toby's sweater. "Cause now you've got dog drool all over you!"

"Eeeeeew, Stephen, what is *wrong* with you?" Toby screamed. "Mom! Mom! Stephen wiped Trusty's drool all over me!"

"That's enough, you two!" his mother called from the kitchen.

•

Stephen walked toward the kitchen, and Trusty followed slowly behind, his collar jingling as it rubbed his stout neck. He opened the refrigerator door. *No,* he told himself, his eyes falling on the bottles of Stella Artois that lined the top shelf of the refrigerator. His fingers fell on the carton of orange juice, but immediately returned to the neck of the beer bottle. "Just one," he told Trusty. Trusty lifted his brown ears slightly, and then settled down on the tile of the floor with a humph.

•

"Do you think there's any dogs in Heaven?" Toby asked Stephen, his brown eyes wide with wonder as he scratched Trusty underneath his new, red collar and watched the young dog's nimble, slender back leg shake involuntarily.

"I don't know," Stephen shot back. "Why would you want to know *that* anyway?" He stared at the screen where his video game car raced through the streets of the city. "You're not still sick, are you?" He paused his game and looked over at where Toby and Trusty lay on the giant red bean bag on the floor.

"No," Toby said. "I'm not sick anymore. Today..." he paused and placed his slender right arm behind his back, crossed his fingers, and continued. "Today," he paused to take a labored breath and then continued again, "the doctor said I'm going to be just fine. The doctor said not to worry at all. He said that my hair will all grow back just in time for our ninth birthday. It's going to come back really long and blond, like Link's hair in *Legend of Zelda*."

"I knew it," Stephen said confidently. He smiled at Toby, who smiled back widely at him, and then he un-paused his game and continued to race through the streets.

•

"This house," Stephen slurred, bending down to scratch Trusty's ear as he placed the fifth bottle of Stella in the recycling container next to the garage door, "has too many ghosts living in it…and not *enough people*!" he called out to no one, enunciating the last two words in the silence of the large, empty house. Trusty lifted his ears and knitted the brown spots of his eyebrows together. He let out a low howl as Stephen picked back up his duffle bag and laundry, closed the door behind him, and stumbled back out into the dark night. Trusty listened as the car roared to life and headed back out the driveway before he settled back down into the muffled silence of the dog bed and thought of the noisy days when the house was filled with laughter and running footsteps. Before the smell of sickness descended upon the little one and eventually permeated through the whole house, and then the whispers filled the bedrooms behind the doors, and then the doors started slamming, and the food dish was filled later and later. He drifted off, his tired, arthritic hindquarter twitching slightly as his old mind dreamed of the days when the two boys would take turns rubbing his belly right in the

sweet spot below his ribs and scratching him behind his ears.

Chapter 33

Jennifer revived, blinking slowly, on the floor of Charles Sewell's office. She was aware of the same haze that surrounded her when she first arrived in the expiation zone, but the dim lighting of the office was unlike the stark white of the E.Z. Rising up, she rubbed her neck with her dainty fingers, and she then looked down on the floor where the gruesome pictures of the accident lay scattered on the ground. She knelt down again to collect them, her eyes taking in the placid, peaceful dark of her lips, the lashes that softened the tranquil eyes, closed as if in an easy sleep right there on the firmness of the city street. She examined each picture earnestly. What was it that she was seeing in the lifeless countenance of the young woman in this graphic account of death, and why did it look so much like happiness?

Suddenly, the jingle of the bells above the door stirred her, and Charles returned to the office, throwing his raincoat over the coat holder and walking over to Bonnie. "Did you have the time to finalize those documents for me?" he asked, walking over to where the woman sat, hunched over a computer keypad.

"I'm just wrapping these up now, *Mr. Sewell*," Bonnie said smiling. She clicked a few buttons on the keyboard, and the printer next to her buzzed to life. "Not to put too fine a point on it, Chuckie, but this proposed plant is awfully close to the town, don't you think?" Bonnie inquired, as she removed the last of the papers from the printer, put a paperclip around them, and then handed them over to Charles. She removed her reading glasses and began cleaning them with her cardigan. "I'm no engineer or environmental expert, but my son and his family don't live more than a mile from it. It's right next to the ballpark where the little league games are. Do you really think that's safe?"

"It doesn't matter what I think, Bonnie," Charles said, dismissively, taking the small stack of papers and heading back into his office. He closed the door behind him and began loosening his tie as he walked. "That woman has got to learn to mind her own business," he remarked to himself, tossing the small stack of papers onto the table. Jennifer inched closer to the man, trying to read over his shoulder. One word stood out among the dense, unfamiliar jargon of the cover page of the document: Solugrid.

"What on Earth?" Jennifer said aloud as she squinted her eyes to get a better look at the writing on the page. "Technical Proposal, New Castle, Pennsylvania, Solugrid Industries." She continued to examine the paper as much as she could over Charles' shoulder, waiting for him to make a move so that she could get a better view. She inched closer but was interrupted by the intercom on Charles' desk.

"Mr. Sewell?" Bonnie's voice crackled through the phone speaker. "I have someone here from the police department."

Charles pressed the button on the intercom. "Send him in, please."

Jennifer moved into the shadows of the room, forgetting that no one could see her. She watched as a middle-aged woman dressed in a dark gray law enforcement uniform with her straw-colored hair pulled back tightly into a bun strode into Charles' office. "Oh, send *her* in," Charles fumbled, rising up from his desk to greet the woman. "My mistake! Please, sit down...Officer...what was your name?"

"Lieutenant Midas," the woman corrected him.

"Uh huh," Charles muttered, reddening. "Well, thank you so much for coming by my office today, Lieutenant Midas. Maybe you're aware, there's some discrepancies in the case file on a homicide by vehicle incident that occurred recently in Youngstown, Ohio." At this, Jennifer peeked out from her place in the shadows and inched closer to where the two stood around Charles' desk, the hair on her arms standing on end. "Commissioner Pusky has asked me to look into it...you know Commissioner Pusky, don't you, Miss—Lieutenant Midas? Please, please, sit down."

Janet Midas looked at Charles with disinterest and grudgingly sat down on a chair that he had pulled out for her on the other side of his desk.

She had been on the department in New Castle for sixteen years, and in that time, she had to fight her way to earn the rank of lieutenant after years of being passed over by her male counterparts. She took her job seriously, and she was keenly aware of the misogynistic Commissioner Pusky and his less than sterling reputation when it came to corruption in Lawrence County. "I...uh...you'll have to excuse me...I thought they would be sending Terry Billings over to look into this case."

"Sergeant Billings does not possess the seniority or expertise in the field of internal investigations that I have, Mr. Sewell. Given the fact that Commisioner Pusky's son has been involved in a case of vehicular manslaughter—"

"Let me...let me stop you there, Officer Midas—"

"Lieutenant Midas—"

"Ok, Lieutenant Midas...I'm sure you're aware that in Pennsylvania, there needs to be positive proof that the driver played a direct and substantial factor in the death of the victim."

"Yes, sir," Lieutenant Midas countered coldly. "As was the case when Mr. Pusky allegedly struck the victim with this vehicle—in Ohio."

"Well…let's not get ahead of ourselves here, Lieutenant Midas," Charles said, reaching for the folder that was on his desk. "I've got some information that might indicate that Stephen Pusky is innocent of criminal negligence and that the victim, Miss…let me see here," he flipped through some pages. "Miss Uccello's actions alone were the sole contributor to her rather unfortunate demise, may she rest in peace."

"Excuse me?"

"Well, according to the information I've got here in this case file…photographic evidence and phone records corroborate that Miss Uccello was engaged in dangers inherent in distraction while acting as a pedestrian on the evening of the accident. Ergo, Mr. Pusky was not at fault in the death of the victim."

Lieutenant Midas's eyes narrowed. "You're trying to tell me that you want Commissioner Pusky's son exonerated because this girl was on a cell phone when he hit her with his car?" she asked incredulously, her voice measured.

"That's correct, Ma'am," Mr. Sewell asserted. "On a cell phone and walking outside the marked crosswalk area. I've got all the evidence that I need right here," he said, tapping the stack of papers against his desk. "Stephen Pusky is innocent of vehicular manslaughter. Now, I hope I didn't take up too much of your time, Miss Midas. Thank you for coming down." He rose suddenly and gestured for Lieutenant Midas to do the same. "If you see Terry down at the precinct today, please tell him I said hello and to stop by if he gets a chance. I'd like to catch up with him."

Janet looked at the stack of papers in Charles' hands. She then sized up Charles from head to toe. "It must be nice to be a friend of yours, Mr. Sewell. It's a shame that poor girl in the photographs wasn't afforded the same luxury. How convenient it is that the law will likely base its judgment on some phone records and photographs and will never hear her side of the story."

From her hiding place behind the door, Jennifer looked forlornly at Lieutenant Midas. She seemed to understand. *My side of the story.* She wracked her brain for it, but that part of her memory was as black and cold as the street below her in the grainy crime scene photos. *My side of the story is gone.*

Chapter 34

Dear Leroy,

I've been meaning to sit down and write you a letter for quite some time. It seems people don't write letters anymore, but I find there's something so nice about the exchange of one person's space for another's when one sits and reads something that someone, somewhere else has hand-written. That's why I wanted to thank you for the beautiful postcards and letters that you sent me over the years while you were away. I would hold them, and for a minute or two, I could be wherever you were...and you were with me in the room while I was reading them. I would always bring the postcards in and show them to my students, and they could never believe how much beauty there was to be found right here in the United States. They liked the colorful pictures on the fronts. I would marvel at the backs and smile at the way you wrote your "i"s and "s"s and remember what it was like when you were just a little boy, holding a pencil and learning to write for the first time. I remember how meticulous I wanted you to be, and how you just wanted to trace the letters as fast as you could so you could run out to the stables and play outside with the horses and sharecroppers. I guess Mama should have known then that it was going to be impossible to tie you down and get you to settle even long enough to eat breakfast. Still, those were some golden times, Leroy. I was so fortunate to be your older sister. I should have cherished it more, but we always seem to want those younger than us to grow up so that they can be as miserable as we are. I wanted you to listen and behave—not giggle and play all day. Now that I've lived long enough, I see that we should all try to spend our lives being as young as the youngest among us. Listening and behaving is how you get old like I am now—and how I've felt my whole life—even when I wasn't old. But...what do I know? What do I know about that?

Can you believe I'll be 97 next month? That would put you at 90 years old. I can't believe it. My baby brother—a nonagenarian! It seems like yesterday that you and Bixby and I were running in the fields together playing hide-and-go-seek. Ha! Isn't that what life is sometimes? Hiding? Hiding from the phone calls we don't want to answer. Or the bills we don't want to pay? Or from fear of an uncertain future. Are we hiding from pain? Hiding from feelings? Hiding from whatever it is that has us scared? And then seeking. Always seeking. I guess that was what you were always doing on your journey with Helios. Seeking. Perhaps it's nice that at a young age, we learn to make a game of the lifelong cycle of closing our eyes and holding things in—and then going and looking for something. I suppose the difference is that kids always find what or who it is that they're looking for. Maybe because they know what they're looking for—even if they don't know exactly where to look. As adults, we tell ourselves that we know the way, but we have no idea who or what it is that we're actually seeking out. We get upset if we don't get exactly what we think we want—even if it's the wrong thing. Kids can just run through the fields, calling out, and if someone is done hiding—out they come! If only the things that we search for in our lives as adults were as open to our calls. If only we were as open to their arrivals.

I feel a sensation as I write this, Leroy. At 96, it's a statistical probability that any day could be my last. I have a greater chance of dying than living, I suppose. I don't mean it in a macabre way—it's just a mathematical certainty. Does a person feel death the way they feel things like fear? Or love? Or anger? The feeling is different. Maybe what's most important is if we feel life. Did you feel life, Leroy? It always looked like you did in the letters and postcards, but I never got to see it in your face or your eyes to be sure. Where was it hiding when you went looking? Did you feel it in the mountains in Colorado? In the picture on the postcard, the sky was purple and orange and pink and blue all at once, and the mountains shot up among the snow with such purpose. Purpose—in spite of all the cold around them. I never could be sure if you were feeling life because your letters and postcards always said that nothing felt like home yet. I hope you felt it. I certainly do hope that you got to feel what it's like to feel at home...that whatever you were looking for was there when you went running after it.

I don't know where to send this letter, Leroy. One day, the postcards and letters just stopped, and the phone didn't ring anymore, and that old feeling I'd get in my heart around springtime started to fade. Especially all these decades later. Maybe I'll seal it up, cover my eyes under the old magnolia tree, and count to 100, waiting for you to come out from hiding...from wherever you've been hiding these past 50 years. Or...if this sensation is right...maybe I will find you sooner than later. There was that giant, gnarled apple tree down by the river where Daddy hung the tire. I used to find you there more often than not. It was your favorite hiding spot. I think...maybe if Heaven is like it is here... I think that might be the first place I'll look. "Olly olly oxen free...ready or not, here I come."

I love you always.

Your sister,

Florence

•

The bells of St. Christine's Roman Catholic Church filled the early spring air, and the red buds began peeking out of their hiding spots on the trees. Bruce Uccello coasted into a parking spot near the grass and pulled up the gear lever of the old Caprice to put it in park. He looked at the line of black-clad people making their way into the church. Some faces were familiar, some not. He watched his ex-wife walk solemnly through the doors, her shoulders drooping with the weight of sadness. She looked older, maybe thinner, but still the same. He watched his ex-brother-in-law wrap an arm around her and lead her inside the narthex to where he couldn't see her anymore. Old aunts, cousins, and friends milled about the entrance, talking to one another before heading in at the coaxing of the carillon bells and the organ. Bruce watched a young man carry a little girl dressed as a princess uncertainly through the heavy, oak doors. She pointed at the colors on the stained-glass window, and he patted her head and smiled. Bruce wanted to rise and get out of the car to join in with the mourners, but he instead sat, tears welling up in his eyes, as he thought of the last time that he was in this very church. He held a tiny, little baby, dressed in the yellowed lace of the family christening gown. Her dark hair was beginning to curl around her ears, and she slept through the whole Mass, not even making a noise when Father Dominick poured the water over her forehead, a plastic pink rosary clutched in her soft, little paws. He remembered the way she would grip onto anything with those soft, strong little hands. He remembered the night she held his index finger for the last time before he packed up his suitcase and walked out the door one winter night, never to come back.

Bruce sighed heavily and pulled back down on the lever of the column gear shift, listening as it clunked into reverse. He backed out onto the street and continued back on Salem road. *What was I thinking?* he wondered, turning the radio button until it clicked on and Donovon's jangly voice sang softly through the FM oldies station. "...lilacs in her hair...Is she dreaming? Yes, I think so. Is she pretty? Yes, ever so..." Bruce reached for the button and turned it left, opting for the fuzz of the scrambled airwaves instead of the music. *I already said goodbye to Jennifer a long time ago. Jesus!*

But at the intersection of Sunnybrook Drive, he slammed on the brakes and coaxed the car back into the lot of St. Christine's, where he jammed the car in park again and sobbed as he never had before in his life. That was still his little girl in there. God damn it! That was still his little girl. "Goodbye" is a tricky thing. Sometimes, we are in charge of it. Or so we think. Maybe we're in charge of the words. Maybe we're in charge of the feet as they turn and walk away. Maybe we stop the fingers from dialing, or the songs from playing, or even the tears from falling. But a heart will cling to a dream long, long after the rest of us has said "so long." Place your hand up to it and feel the beats. We think we hear, "Good bye…good bye," but until it finally stops, it is always saying, "Not yet…not yet…not yet…not yet…"

Bruce opened the door of the Caprice, breathed in the spring air, and headed toward the heavy oak door of the church. Inside, he tapped his ex-wife on the shoulder and immediately held her close as she spun around to see him. They stayed like that, not needing to say anything, awash in their common sadness, their two hearts one as they looked upon the little girl who, for better or worse for all of her succinct life, was a product of that.

Chapter 35

Jennifer left Charles' office and walked out to where Bonnie sat knitting at her desk. Jennifer watched as Bonnie adroitly moved the yarn between the two needles, barely looking at them. She watched the scarf take shape row by row from the twists and turns of a pattern that she couldn't see or understand.

"Marty, is that you?" Bonnie called out softly.

Jennifer looked around, not seeing anyone. She moved closer to Bonnie, scanning the room.

"Marty?" Bonnie repeated. She sighed deeply and smiled. "Must be these drafty, old walls again, Marty. I thought it was you stopping by for a visit."

Jennifer continued to survey the room, but she didn't see anything out of order.

"I'm making this scarf for Lucas, see?" Bonnie continued, holding up the scarf. "I know it's almost April, but I figure he could maybe use it next year. You should see him, Marty. Can you? Can you see him?" Jennifer's eyes narrowed, and she stepped away from her position behind Bonnie.

"Well, you'd be proud of him," Bonnie went on. "He's quite the baseball player...just like you were." Jennifer again moved closer to Bonnie, and the elderly woman pulled her cardigan close around her neck. Jennifer moved her fingers through the woman's hair and waved her hands gently in front of the woman's face to see if there would be some reaction.

Can she...?

Bonnie rubbed her arms and shivered. "Jeepers, Marty! Is it cold in here, or are you visiting me? I can never tell anymore...seems like I'm always cold these days. Or maybe you're always visiting! Anyway, like I was saying, Lucas is quite the ball player. I go to his games down at the field to watch him play. It's the same one I used to go see you play in back when we first started courting. It seems like yesterday....Course, Chuckie and his pals are fixing to put up some kinda power plant right behind where we used to go for drives after the games. It's a shame, isn't it, Marty? Everything's changing anymore...faster than I can keep up with. It really is a shame..."

"It doesn't have to be," Jennifer vowed. She looked down at the picture of the little boy in the red baseball uniform on Bonnie's desk and thought of Nox Reyes and his devious company and the way that he stopped at nothing—even in his death—to try to advance his position at Solugrid Industries. His work here was done, but maybe hers wasn't. "It doesn't have to be," she maintained. Jennifer raced back into Charles' office and looked through the confidential file with her information on it, and then she looked at the clock on his desk. It was almost 4 P.M. Most banks, post offices, and businesses would be closing in another hour, and she had only seven more hours remaining in what she had hoped would be her fifth and final day. "How am I supposed to take this information and make it into a positive?" she appealed to the sky.

Immediately, her Nona's voice filled the dark office, echoing the words she had said when Jennifer saw her image in the mirror. *Isn't it nice to know that we are part of something so much bigger than all of us that we're all too small to see it? Make the most of it, Birdie. You've got one more day. Don't just multiply that day by itself and keep it at one. See if you can do something for people that will make it hundreds... Make it millions. You only have one day left...See if you can make it eternity.*

Jennifer scooped up the files on Charles' desk and went back to where Bonnie sat knitting in the front office down the hall corridor. She thought of Patty's insistence that God was in everything, and she felt empowered in her belief that Patty was right. Jennifer had spent her entire time in the Expiation Zone desperately wondering *how* she died. And now, as she stood in the office building of the man who would acquit her killer, poised

to make her final move, she finally understood exactly *why* she did.

Chapter 36

"Bonnie! Bonnie, that meeting starts in ten minutes. Did you make copies of those files that I had on my desk?"

"I sure did, Chuckie. Boy, that was a good idea. Way to stick it to 'em. I knew you'd do the right thing. You know, your great uncle would be really proud of you and the man that you've become."

Charles looked at her quizzically, unsure of what she meant. "That lady is losing her marbles," he muttered under his breath as he picked up the stack of papers from Bonnie's desk and walked out of the office building. Jennifer smiled and followed behind him as he hopped into his black Mercedes S550 and pulled out of the parking lot. She reached down and felt the warm baseball glove leather of the seats. *I always wanted a Mercedes-Benz*, she thought as she closed her eyes and enjoyed the short ride down the block to the town council meeting at the New Castle Borough Building. Charles pushed in the button to park the vehicle, gathered his folders into his black leather briefcase, and closed the quiet door of the car. Jennifer watched as he ascended the ramp and opened the door to the building. The sun peeked out from behind a cloud, and she took a deep breath to settle herself before following in behind him.

The small room had about sixty people in it. Most were clumped together in groups by age. Some looked impressively dressed, others as if they had just come from a hard day of work. Some were talking about paint for the baseball field dugout. An elderly woman with a walker had come with pictures stuffed in her pocketbook showing the water that had backed up into her house as a result of supposed poor drainage. There were a handful of young kids from the local scout troops who were going to be presented badges for learning about fire safety. As Jennifer looked at this mixed group of people, she felt a knot in her throat. She would never grow old enough to come to a meeting like this, complaining about water in her basement. She would never see the excitement of a son's face as his pinewood derby car raced toward the finish line. Here she was on what she had hoped would be the final day of her brief final days. By 26, her marriage had failed, and she spent her nights highlighting and cutting hair, trying to will her heart to forget a pain that it wouldn't let go.

"Please rise for the Pledge of Allegiance before our meeting begins," a man seated in the middle of a table set up in the front of the room began, calling the meeting to order. Jennifer listened to the words that she had recited every day as a girl in school and now breathed each one with heartfelt finality where she once used to drone them by rote. "One nation, under God. Indivisible. With liberty. And justice. For all."

The people in the room sat down, and the man in the center of the table again spoke. "I need a motion to approve the minutes from last month's meeting." He looked around the table and received a nod from another man sitting near the end. "Bob," the man responded, shaking his head. "Second?" A woman next to him raised her hand. "Alice," he affirmed. "Well, I'd like to get started with a proposal that we have from Attorney Charles Sewell. As you may or may not know, Mr. Sewell has been contacted by a global energy firm that has expressed an interest in a large-scale power project that would be housed right here in Lawrence County. He and Commissioner Pusky have been approached by—what is it, Charles? Soledad?"

"Solugrid," Charles said nervously, rising and clearing his throat as he looked around the room of leery faces. "This is all just proposed, I'd like to remind you...but I do have some information that the company would like the board—and, uh...any local residents who would be interested," he added hesitantly. "I can distribute these to you, if you'd like..."

"I'll take one!" one middle-aged man in the crowd said.

"I'd like one, too," agreed the elderly woman with the wet basement.

"Ok, okay...Bob...could you help me hand these out to whomever needs one?"

Charles began hastily handing stapled copies of the sample request for a proposal out to outstretched arms.

"Hey, this wasn't on the agenda!" one man challenged angrily. "When were we going to hear about this one? You guys are always trying to fleece us here in this town. It seems like there's always something shady going on here."

"Yeah...that's right! What about the parking lot fiasco last year?" demanded another voice. "Where'd the money go on that one?"

"This—uh, this is all just preliminary at this point, sir," Charles responded nervously. "If you could all just hold your commentary for the time being and turn to page three..."

A hush fell over the crowd, and the elderly woman gasped as she flipped to the page. Jennifer looked around with a wry grin at the astonished and distraught looks on the faces of the people in the crowd. The board members sitting at the table began to buzz nervously, and the woman whom Jennifer recognized as the one from lunch earlier in the day held a hand up to her chest as her eyes grew wide.

"What...uh...what's going on here?" a confused Charles asked, comparing his original copy of the proposal to that of the man next to him. His face flushed as he stared in horror and saw how on each page, a cut-out image of a pretty, young woman lying lifelessly was juxtaposed next to the reports on engineering, procurement, and construction. The plans for fuel supply and transportation had a similar picture of a deceased young woman, but from another angle. The full photograph with a dark pool welling under the woman's body smeared against the proposed budget schedules. "These—" he stammered. "—These are not on the original..."

"Well, what the hell kind of plant is this you're trying to bring here?" A voice called from the crowd.

"I don't think we need anything in this town that's going to kill us!" said the woman with the wet basement.

"I vote no," Bob declared emphatically. "I didn't like the sound of this at first, and I don't like the look of it now. I vote no to even discussing the prospect of this any further! This," he gestured, holding up the packet, "is not a good sign. And this is not what New Castle needs!"

"I second that!" yelled a voice from the crowd.

The woman who met at lunch was pasty white and incredulous. She met Charles's eyes, and he looked at her in confusion. *What the hell happened?* She mouthed as she watched the angry crowd tear the proposal papers, get up, and walk toward the board table.

I have no idea, he mouthed back, shaking his head and backing away from the swarm that inched nearer to him. "Ladies and gentlemen, please...I assure you...this was all just a proposal. The plant is not a certainty. There's some ordinances that would need to be amended for us to even consider moving forward with the planning—"

"Well, we don't want those amendments!" came a shout from the crowd. "And we don't want this plant!"

Jennifer surveyed the room with integrity. She looked at each face, trying to think of what each story would be and where each would end. Solugrid had lost here, and in some small way, this town had won because of it. Once she had seen the board secretary write that the amendment needed for the proposed plant was refused with a definitive "no" as a result of a majority vote by the council, she walked back outside and strode slowly down the street, looking at the buildings and trees that lined the avenue. She bent down to pick up something from the ground and then continued on her way. Yes, she was just a deceased 26 year-old hairdresser who never had the chance to do the things that she thought that she wanted to do in her life...but it did pay to be handy with the scissors from time to time...and some skill with a copy machine didn't hurt either. Jennifer smiled. Bonnie Sewell,

Jennifer's fifth mission, just changed the course of history for the citizens of her town for the better—and she didn't even know it.

Jennifer walked back into Charles' office, where Bonnie was just putting on her coat and getting ready to turn out the lights.

"Marty?" Bonnie said softly, as she felt a chill come into the room. She turned around to see the red feather that Jennifer had placed next to the picture of her grandson Lucas dressed in his New Castle Cardinals little league baseball uniform. "Awww, Marty," she sighed, a tear rolling down her cheek. "I knew it was you…"

Chapter 37

Jennifer awoke to the sound of birds singing. She looked uncertainly around, and her eyes focused groggily on a giant mountain that seemed to tower in the distance. It soared above the line of silver clouds in the electric blue sky and climbed without apparent end toward the firmament above. She took in the green of the trees and grass around her and the unparalleled beauty of the placid lake in the distance where the sun shimmered and danced in the reflection. She was relieved to see a world bursting with color brighter than she had ever seen—instead of one filled with stark white. For a minute, she was filled with a feeling of the first day of spring. She took a deep breath and let the newness of the spring air permeate throughout her. She exhaled and then breathed deeply again, seeing as if for the first time every detail of her surroundings. She looked around, feeling light as air, wanting to run toward the lake. She felt as if she could fly. She had made it. She had made it! And she had eternity to enjoy this weightless feeling. She looked toward the mountain and again breathed in the pulchritude of life that besieged her, her heart bursting with joyous song. Another vaguely familiar scent edged in on the freshness of spring.

"Lord!" She heard a smooth voice purr from behind her. "I sure hope that bird pipes down soon. I don't want to have to listen to that damned chirping until the end of time."

Jennifer's smile could have held eternity.